ALL GONE

JOHNS HOPKINS: POETRY AND FICTION

John T. Irwin, General Editor

OTHER BOOKS BY STEPHEN DIXON

No Relief (stories), 1976

Work (novel), 1977

Too Late (novel), 1978

Quite Contrary (stories), 1979

Fourteen Stories (stories), 1980

Movies (stories), 1983

Time to Go (stories), 1984

Fall & Rise (novel), 1985

Garbage (novel), 1988

The Play (stories), 1989

Love & Will (stories), 1989

ALL GONE

18 Short Stories

Stephen Dixon

The Johns Hopkins University Press   Baltimore and London

To Barbara Richert and Jerome Klinkowitz,
for their help and encouragement over the years

©1990 The Johns Hopkins University Press
All rights reserved
Printed in the United States of America

The Johns Hopkins University Press
701 West 40th Street, Baltimore, Maryland 21211
The Johns Hopkins Press Ltd., London

This book has been brought to publication with the generous assistance of the
G. Harry Pouder Fund and the Albert Dowling Trust.

The paper used in this publication meets the minimum requirements of
American National Standard for Information Sciences—Permanence of Paper
for Printed Library Materials, ANSI Z39.48-1984.

Library of Congress Cataloging-in-Publication Data
Dixon, Stephen, 1936—
All gone: 18 short stories / Stephen Dixon.
p.   cm.—(Johns Hopkins, poetry and fiction)
ISBN 0-8018-4010-4 (alk. paper)
I. Title. II. Series.
PS3554.I92A44   1990
813'.54—dc20   89-43537 CIP

Permissions appear on p. 152.

CONTENTS

THE STUDENT

This begins more than four years ago. It was when I was driving a cab in the day and going to college at night. I was a pre-dental student. I lived in a single room. My folks were dead. I had no close relatives. I was dating someone and had a number of friends. I had little time for parties and movies though, what with my studying and job. My girlfriend, Louise, usually stayed with me weekends. We planned to get married during my third year of dental school, when she'd be graduated and teaching second grade.

One Saturday, when Louise was studying her own college work in my room, I was driving a man through the factory part of the city. I suddenly felt this cold thing on the back of my neck. I swatted it from behind. The thing came right back to the same spot. "It's a gun," the man said. "Make another move it doesn't like and it'll bite off your head."

"I'll do anything you say," I said.

"That's a smart hack."

"You want all my money, you can have it."

"Just stick to your driving."

"You want me to still drive to where you asked to go?"

"Drive around this block."

"And after that?"

"Just keep driving around this block."

He took the gun away from my neck. In the rearview mirror I saw him sitting in the middle of the back seat. He was nicely

dressed in an overcoat, suit, tie and hat. His gloved hands held
the gun between his knees and kept it pointing up at me.

I drove around the block several times.

"How many times you want me to drive around the block?"
I said.

"Till I say for you to stop."

"And if I run out of gas?"

"No funny remarks."

"That wasn't intended to be funny. I'm low."

"You'll be lower if you make any more funny remarks."

"I mean I'm very low in gas. I was going to get a few dollars'
worth right after I dropped you off."

"You'll be dropping off if you don't shut up fast."

I drove around the same block about two dozen times. The
gun was still between his knees. Just the end of the barrel was
visible now and still pointing at my head. Then the cab began
making these bumping back and forth movements every few seconds.

"What's that?" he said.

"That's the gas tank going out of gas."

"I'm serious. What is it?"

"You must have never owned a car. Take a look at the
gauge."

"Then get to a garage fast."

I told him I knew of one right around here. It was cold
outside and all the windows were up but mine, which was opened
just an inch. And there was no glass partition or steel cage sep-
arating the driver from the passenger section, as all the fleet cabs
in the city are forced by law to have now. Not that a thick glass
or cage would have stopped any caliber bullet from coming into
me from behind, if I had wanted to yell for help through my
window crack or signal with my hand or lights to a policeman
if I saw one nearby.

"And no funny remarks or lowering the window an inch
more or getting out of the cab," the man said, putting the gun
in an overcoat side pocket, "or the trigger gets touched. It's a
hair trigger too."

I wanted to ask him what exactly a hair trigger was, something I read of in newspapers and heard said about in movies

and never looked up, but I knew he would think that a funny remark. Or maybe I wasn't as calm as all that and only imagined I wanted to ask him that question. Later on though, I told people I had asked him what a hairpin trigger was and that he said "It's a trigger that releases the hammer that strikes the cartridge primer that sends the bullet up through the back of a cabby's head and out of his hair like a pin."

I drove the few blocks to the gas station and pulled up beside the gas pumps.

"Seven dollars of the cheaper grade," I told the attendant, "and a receipt."

"Why'd you ask for a receipt?" the man said when the attendant began putting in gas.

"I always get a receipt when I don't fill up at the taxi garage."

"No receipt," he said.

"But I need a receipt to get my seven dollars back. I've dealt with this guy. He knows that."

"I don't want you passing anything to him."

"What could I pass? He'll be the one passing me the receipt."

"No."

"That's seven dollars," the attendant said.

I gave him a ten.

"I'll get your change and receipt."

"No receipt," the man said to me.

"No receipt," I yelled to the attendant as he headed for the station office.

"It's no trouble," he said.

"No thanks."

"No three dollars either," the man said.

"I shouldn't wait for my three dollars?" I said.

"Get going."

"Forget the three dollars also," I yelled to the attendant as he left the office.

"But I got it right here."

"We're in a rush. Sorry."

"Sorry for what? Are you kidding?"

"Why'd you tell him we're in a rush?" the man said.

"I said what came into my head."

"Stupid."

"Really," the attendant said. "Three bucks tip is crazy," and he held the three dollars through the window space.

"Should I take it?" I said to the man in back.

"Why you asking me?"

"Is it yours?" the attendant said to him, his mouth at my window and waving the money through the space to the man. "Well really thanks, mister, but three dollars is a pretty large tip."

"Will you please take your change?" the man said. "Because I am in a rush."

"I'll take it," I said to the attendant.

"I shouldn't have said anything," he said. "Three dollars would have done me fine."

"Now please get moving," the man said, pointing to his watch.

"See you," I said to the attendant and drove out of the station. "Where you want to go now?"

"Around this block," the man said.

"This block?"

"You see another block?"

"There are lots of blocks around here. This, that and all the other blocks including the factory one we must have driven around a hundred times. It's a big neighborhood. An even bigger city."

"Shut your mouth and drive." He took the gun from his pocket and held it between his knees.

I drove around the block that had the gas station on the corner of it. The first time the attendant saw me he waved. He waved the second time also and then scratched his head when he saw me coming a third and fourth time. The fifth time he saw me he yelled "Hey, you're driving in circles." I shrugged. The man in the back said "Don't shrug. Don't make faces. Behave like your driving is perfectly normal." The next time the attendant saw me he yelled "You're getting me dizzy with your driving—you know that?" The time after that, he was pointing out my cab to a driver of another car in the gas station and yelling "What's your cab—locked to hidden street rails we don't know about?" Then he gave up on saying anything to me and only made the crazy sign with his finger screwing away at his temple, and the times after that he mostly wouldn't even look up.

We drove around the same block for about a half hour. Finally I said "You still want me to drive around this block?"

"Yes."

"That gas station guy's going to get suspicious."

"That's his trouble."

"He could call the police thinking something's wrong."

"Then that's their trouble."

"The police could try to stop us and you might use your gun on them and they might use their guns on you and I could get killed in the crossfire."

"What do you know?—Just keep driving."

"Why don't we drive around another block? One away from the gas station."

"This block."

"We drove around another block before."

"That was till you ran out of gas."

"I could run out of gas again. This stop-and-go driving drains the hell out of it."

"Then you'll get some more at the station."

"What could I ever say to that man the next time?"

"You'll say 'Fill her up, please, and no receipt.' And then exchange pleasantries about cars, auto parts and motor oils, or just read from one of the books on your seat."

"You must like that gas station very much."

"Save your remarks for the gas pumper."

"I will. I was just trying to be protective about myself then. I don't want to get hurt or cause any trouble in the least."

The gun was still pointing at me. I drove around the block another fifteen minutes. Every three times around or so the attendant looked at me and went right back to his work. Then I saw a policeman waving me down on the avenue around the block from the gas station.

"Keep driving around the block," the man said.

"But he wants me to stop."

"Pass him the next time you see him too."

"He'll have a car on our tail by then."

"Do as I say."

I drove past the policeman. Through the side mirror I saw him calling out for me to stop. Through the rearview mirror I saw the man putting the gun in his overcoat pocket. We passed the gas station. The attendant was wiping someone's dipstick. We went around the block. The policeman ran farther into the avenue this time and waved his nightstick for me to stop.

"The light's red," I said, passing the policeman.

"Go through it and around the block again and then stop where he says stop."

"Why not back up for him now? I could say I didn't see him the first time because I was keeping my eyes out for a certain address, and only saw him the second time when I was turning the corner and had mistakenly gone through the light."

He motioned me to continue around the block.

"You're the one asking for trouble now," I said.

"From you?"

"From the police. I could still back all the way up this block and around to where he is. It'll look better for us if I come around backward that way. More respectful, and as if I only passed him once and not twice."

"Shhh."

I drove around the block. The policeman was calling in from a police box on a lamppost. Seeing the cab, he dropped the receiver and blew his whistle at me. I stopped. He started over to us.

"Roll up your window," the man said.

I rolled it up. "What do I tell him when he gets here?"

"Cover your mouth when you talk to me now and don't turn around."

I put my hand over my mouth and said without turning around "Well, what do I?"

"Tell him you drove through the lights and didn't stop when he told you to because you wanted to help him lose some fat by his chasing after you."

I shook my head.

"Say what I said."

The policeman rapped my window with his stick. "Roll it down."

"Three inches," the man said.

I rolled it down three inches.

"Anything wrong in there?" the policeman asked the man.

"Nothing, thank you."

"Now let's hear you start explaining this," the policeman said to me.

"I'm very sorry, officer."

"What about what you ordered me to say about him?" the man said.

"What he order you?" the policeman said.

"I think he should be the one to say it."

"That I only passed you because I wanted you to run a ways after me so you could lose a little weight."

"Get out," the policeman said.

"Do I?" I said into my hand without turning around.

"You're damn right you'll get out," the policeman said.

"I don't know what to do," I told him. I covered my mouth and said "What do I do?"

The policeman unsnapped his holster flap and tried opening the door. In the rearview the man made a turning motion with his hand for me to roll my window up.

"No need, officer," I said, when he tried opening the rear door. "I'm coming out."

He stepped back, his hand on his holstered gun. I rolled up my window. He smashed my window with his stick.

The man slunk back into his seat screaming and then said "Get."

I drove off. Some glass had got in my cheek. The policeman shot once into the air. Then two more.

"Drive to the block with the movie theater on it," the man said, pointing to a movie theater a few blocks away.

"And the light?"

"No. This block here with the supermarket. Keep driving around it and don't stop for police or lights."

I drove through the red light and started around the block. We were on the avenue in front of the market completing our third trip around the block when I saw two police cars waiting for me in my lane.

"Make a U," he said.

I made a U-turn and then a left at the first side street as he told me to do.

"Which block?" I said.

"Find another one around here. But a big one. If possible

a block with the city's biggest avenues on opposite ends of it."

"There aren't any around here like that."

"Then drive across the park to the south side. I know of a beauty over there, right off Fourth."

I drove across town and was heading south through the park transverse when I saw that both lanes ahead were blocked with police cars.

"Around," he said, but through the side mirror I could see that the way back was blocked too.

"What now?" I said, slowing down.

"Get out and run."

I stopped the cab between the two police car blockades and said "If I run they might shoot me."

"And if you don't run I'll shoot you. And if you do run and suddenly stop I'll shoot you. And if you fall to the ground after you get out and suddenly stop I'll shoot you. I'll shoot you if you try climbing over the transverse wall or get out and yell to the police and me not to shoot you. Just get out and run either way down the road's dividing line to the police shouting threats that you're going to kill them, or I'll shoot you from behind. Now out," and he nudged the gun barrel against the back of my neck.

I got out, jumped to the ground and crawled underneath the cab. He began shooting through the floor. Two bullets hit my shoulder and arm, another ricocheted through my ear. The police drove up. They called out to me. They took the gun from the man and asked him why he had shot me. Shaking all over and between loud sobs and tears he said "This bum . . . this man . . . he forced me to drive with him as a hostage. I luckily disarmed him of that thing seconds before he was going to drive us straight into your cars and shoot every policeman he could see."

Even with two bullets and glass in me and blood coming out of my face and clothes, a policeman wrenched my head back by the hair and threw me against the cab and slammed my handcuffed hands on the hood and kicked my feet out behind me and told me to keep my legs spread apart and don't speak unless questioned or they'll knock me to the ground for good.

"But the man's lying. I was his hostage and was forced to drive around and taunt you guys."

I was punched in the back and head by two policemen till I rolled off the hood to the ground.

The man and I were driven in separate cars to the police station. An hour after I was arraigned and exhibited to the press for photographs, I was taken to the hospital, where my bullet and glass wounds were treated and also a gash in the back of my head that the policeman's ring had opened up.

I was brought to trial. My court-appointed lawyer advised me to stop repeating those ridiculous statements about the man forcing me to do all those things in my cab.

"He's a university professor," the lawyer said. "Has written several highly regarded textbooks on forensic psychiatry and medicine. And he and his wife have such an impeccable reputation and social standing in the city that he could never be thought to have done the bizarre things you claim. I don't believe you. The judge certainly won't believe you. The prosecuting attorney is too good for the jury to believe you. If you plead guilty to all charges and ask the court's mercy, I can get you off with only a few years. If you don't plead guilty, then the professor and that policeman and gas station attendant will testify against you and you can be sent away for thirty years."

I pleaded guilty and got six years. In prison I was taught mess hall cooking and worked in the kitchen there the last three years of my term. In the prison library I read as many books on psychology and psychiatry, including two of the professor's works, as any student could read in any university in the world.

Lots of times in prison I thought about getting revenge on that man once I got out. I thought I would wait for him outside his class, and only after I was sure he remembered me and the ride we took together, would I slam a two-by-four over his head, not caring if he got killed. But then I knew I could never do anything that fierce. So I thought I'd just walk up to him on the street and slap his face, and after I wrestled him to the ground, as he was a pretty small guy so probably easy to handle, I'd kick his legs and arms and maybe spit at him, and then just leave him there like that.

But I knew I wouldn't be capable of doing any of those things either. After reading those psychology and psychiatry books, I found I wasn't at all the type to go around kicking and slapping anyone for anything. I also learned from those books that the professor was the type who would always have a gun, or know where to get one, and that he would come after me and use it if I so much as accused him of the crimes I went to prison for and took a swing at his face. And he'd have all the right excuses too. He could say "That man tried to kill me for having told the truth about that day he kept me captive in his cab. For he swore to me in the cab that he'd get even with me if I ever talked. And he's phoned me a number of times since he left prison, with threats against my wife and me. So I got a gun. All right—I got it illegally"—if he couldn't get it legally and as the one he had in the cab must have been gotten—"but I was desperately afraid of him. And when he came for me I had to shoot him to save my life."

So I gave up on getting revenge. I was a model prisoner, got out in four years and returned to college, but this time to get a simple business degree in restaurant management. Louise, my old girlfriend, was too seriously involved with someone else to see me. Some of my old friends were still in the city. They all had fairly good jobs and a couple of them were married and had children. The few times I did meet some of them for beers, they asked me to tell the story about the professor and me. But I always told them it was best for my future career and personal well-being if I forgot that incident forever and if everybody else forgot about it too.

Most nights now I worked as a waiter. About once a week since I got the job a few months ago, that same man comes in the restaurant and sits at my station and orders drinks and a complete meal. Near the end of his dinner on the first night, he said "Aren't you the fellow who did that strange thing with the taxi and police that was such a popular news story a few years ago?"

I said "I'm the man, all right," and he said "I thought you looked familiar. You've clipped most of your hair and taken to wearing a mustache and eyeglasses, but I suppose those pictures of you on TV and in the papers left an indelible impression on me. I happen to have more than a morbid gossiper's concern in criminal cases and yours I have to admit was one of the more interesting ones." Then he excused himself for having brought up the subject, "since it must be embarrassing if not potentially damaging to you for anyone to repeat it in public," and didn't say another word to me for the rest of the meal except "Thank you" and "Goodbye."

Since then, after his first drink, he always asks if I'd mind speaking some more about that day he had talked about, and I always say I wouldn't.

"What I'm saying," he's said in a different way each time, "is I don't want you getting mad at me or anything. Because if you think I'm being nosey, even if it is with a professional interest in mind that could lead to a paper on the subject, please say so and I'll shut up and never ask you about it again."

He always asks just one question each dinner, though a different one each time. Such as "What prompted your doing it in the first place?" and "Didn't you think you could get killed in the act?" and "Where did you get the courage to face the police like that?" and "What was the significance of riding around the blocks so many times?" and "Why for a while did you settle on just one gas station in case you ran out of gas a second time?" and "Didn't you know that if caught you'd be jeopardizing your employment and social activities for life?" and "Did you really believe you were innocent as you first proclaimed to the press the day you were caught?" and "Didn't it occur to you that your passenger might have been killed by the police for being thought of as your accomplice or by a stray bullet aimed at you?"

I always make up an answer for him. Such as "At the time I intentionally wanted to get myself killed," and "I really can't say why I did anything that day because it was essentially another me who was responsible for the act," and "I went around and around those blocks to draw attention to myself, simple as that," and "I was too concerned with carrying out the crime itself and having a good time playing around with the police to pay any attention to the passenger in back."

My answer always seems to satisfy him for the time. He then apologizes for having brought up the subject again and changes the conversation by asking after my health or college work or if the dinner special looks good tonight, and throughout the rest of the meal acts somewhat frightened as if he thinks I'm about to pick up a chair and crash it down on him. Then he finishes his dinner and the bottle of wine he always orders with his meal, and leaves without ever giving me a tip.

ALL GONE

He says goodbye, we kiss at the door, he rings for the elevator, I say "I'll call you when I find out about the tickets," he says "Anytime, as I'll be in all day working on that book jacket I'm behind on," waves to me as the elevator door opens and I shut the door.

I find out about the tickets and call him and he doesn't answer. Maybe he hasn't gotten home yet, though he usually does in half an hour. But it's Saturday and the subway's always much slower on weekends, and I call him half an hour later and he doesn't answer.

He could have got home and I missed him because he right away might have gone out to buy some necessary art supply or something, and I call him an hour later and he doesn't answer. I do warm-ups, go out and run my three miles along the river, come back and shower and call him and he doesn't answer. I dial him every half hour after that for the next three hours and then call Operator and she checks and says his phone's in working order.

I call his landlord and say "This is Maria Pierce, Eliot Schulter's good friend for about the last half-year—you know me. Anyway, could you do me a real big favor and knock on his door? I know it's an inconvenience but he's only one flight up and you see, he should be home and doesn't answer and I've been phoning and phoning him and am getting worried. I'll call you back in fifteen minutes. If he's in and for his own reasons didn't want to answer the phone or it actually is out of order, could you have him call me at home?"

I call the landlord back in fifteen minutes and he says "I did what you said and he didn't answer. That would've been enough for me. But you got me worried also, so I went downstairs for his duplicate keys and opened his door just a ways and yelled in for him and then walked in and he wasn't there, though his place looked okay."

"Excuse me, I just thought of something. Was his night light on?"

"You mean the little small-watt-bulb lamp on his fireplace mantel?"

"That's the one. He always keeps it on at night to keep away burglars who like to jump in from his terrace."

"What burglars jumping in from where? He was never robbed that I know."

"The tenant before him said she was. Was it on?"

"That's different. Yes. I thought he'd forgotten about the light, so I shut it off. I was thinking about his electricity cost, but you think I did wrong?"

"No. It only means he never got home. Thanks."

I call every half hour after that till around six, when he usually comes to my apartment. But he never comes here without our first talking on the phone during the afternoon about all sorts of things: how our work's going, what the mail brought, what we might have for dinner that evening and do later and if there's anything he can pick up on the way here and so on. The concert's at eight and I still have to pick up the tickets from my friend who's giving them to me and can't go herself because her baby's sick and her husband won't go without her. I call her and say "I don't see how we can make the concert. Eliot's not here, hasn't called, doesn't answer his phone and from what his landlord said, I doubt he ever got home after he left me this morning."

"Does he have any relatives or close friends in the city for you to call?"

"No, he would have gone to his apartment directly—I know him. He had important work to finish, and the only close person other than myself to him is his mother in Seattle."

"Maybe he did get home but got a very sudden call to drop everything and fly out to her, so he didn't have the time to phone you, or when he did, your line was busy."

"No, we're close enough that he'd know it would worry me. He'd have called from the airport, someplace."

"Your line still could have been busy all the times you were trying to get him. But I'm sure everything's okay, and don't worry about the tickets. Expensive as they are, I'll put them down as a total loss. Though if you are still so worried about him, phone the police in his neighborhood or even his mother in Seattle."

"Not his mother. There's no reason and I'd just worry her and Eliot would get angry at me. But the police is a good idea."

I call the police station in his precinct. The officer who answers says "We've nothing on a Mr. Schulter. But being that you say he left your apartment this morning, phone your precinct station," and she gives me the number. I call it and the officer on duty says "Something did come in today about someone of his name—let me think."

"Oh no."

"Hey, take it easy. It could be nothing. I'm only remembering that I saw an earlier bulletin, but what it was went right past me. What's your relationship to him before I start searching for it?"

"His closest friend. We're really very very close and his nearest relative is three thousand miles from here."

"Well, I don't see it in front of me. I'll locate it, though don't get excited when I'm away. It could be nothing. I might even be wrong. It was probably more like a Mr. Fullter or Schulton I read about, but not him. Want me to phone you back?"

"I'll wait, thanks."

"Let me take your number anyway, just in case I get lost."

He goes, comes back in a minute. "Now take it easy. It's very serious. He had no I.D. on him other than this artist society card with only his signature on it, which we were checking into, so we're grateful you called."

"Please, what is it?"

"According to this elderly witness, he was supposedly thrown on the subway tracks this morning and killed."

I scream, break down, hang up, pound the telephone table

with my fists, the officer calls back and says "If you could please revive yourself, Miss, we'd like you to come to the police station here and then, if you could by the end of the night sometime, to the morgue to identify your friend."

I say no, I could never go to the morgue, but then go with my best friend. She stays outside the body room when I go in, look and say "That's him." Later I call Eliot's mother and the next day her brother comes to the city and takes care of the arrangements to have Eliot flown to Seattle and his apartment closed down and most of his belongings sold or given away or put on the street. The uncle asks if I'd like to attend the funeral, but doesn't mention anything about providing air fare or where I would stay. Since I don't have much money saved and also think I'll be out of place there and maybe even looked down upon by his family I've never seen, I stay here and arrange on that same funeral day a small ceremony in the basement of a local church, where I and several of our friends and his employers speak about Eliot and read aloud excerpts of his letters to a couple of us and listen to parts of my opera records he most liked to play and for a minute bow our heads, hold hands and pray.

According to that elderly witness, Eliot was waiting for a train on the downtown platform of my stop when he saw a young man speaking abusively to a girl of about fifteen. When the girl continued to ignore him, he made several obscene gestures and said he was going to throw her to the platform and force her to do all sorts of sordid things to him and if he couldn't get her to do them there because people were watching, then in the men's room upstairs. The girl was frightened and started to walk away. The young man grabbed her wrist, started to twist it, stopped and said he would rip her arm off if she gave him a hard time, but didn't let go. There were a few people on the platform. Nobody said anything or tried to help her and in fact all of them except Eliot and this elderly man eventually moved to the other end of the platform or at least away from what was going on. Then Eliot went over to the young man, who was still holding the girl by her wrist, and very politely asked him to let her alone. Something like "Excuse me, I don't like to interfere in anyone's problems. But if this young lady doesn't want to be bothered by you, then I would really think you'd let her go."

"Listen, I know her, so mind your business," the young man said and she said to Eliot "No he don't." Then out of nowhere a friend of the young man ran down the subway stairs and said to him "What's this chump doing, horning in on your act?" The elderly man got up from a bench and started for the upstairs to get help. "You stay right here, grandpa," the first young man said, "or you'll get thrown on your back too." The elderly man stopped. Eliot said to the young men "Please, nobody should be getting thrown on their backs. And I hate to get myself any more involved in this, but for your own good you fellows ought to go now or just leave everybody here alone."

"And for your own good," one of the young men said, "you'd be wiser moving your ass out of here."

"I can only move it once I know this girl's out of danger with you two."

"She'll be plenty out of danger when you move your ass out of here, now move."

"Believe me, I'd like to, but how can I? Either you leave her completely alone now or I'll have to get the police."

That's when they jumped him, beat him to the ground and, when he continued to fight back with his feet, fists and butting his head, picked him up and threw him on the tracks. He landed on his head and cracked his skull and something like a blood clot suddenly shot through to the brain, a doctor later said. The girl had already run away. The young men ran the opposite way. The elderly man shouted at Eliot to get up, then at people to jump down to the tracks to help Eliot up, then ran in the direction the young men went to the token booth upstairs and told the attendant inside that an unconscious man was lying on the tracks and for her to do something quick to prevent a train from running over him. She phoned from the booth. He ran back to the platform and all the way to the other end of it yelling to the people around him "Stop the train. Man on the tracks, stop the local train." When the downtown local entered the station a minute later, he and most of the people along the platform screamed and waved the motorman to stop the train because someone was on the tracks. The train came to a complete stop ten feet from Eliot. A lot of the passengers were thrown to the floor and the next few days a number of them sued the city for the dizzy spells and sprained fingers and ripped clothes they said they got from the sudden train stop and also for the days and weeks they'd have to miss from their jobs because of their injuries. Anyway, according to that same doctor who examined Eliot at the hospital, he was dead a second or two after his head hit the train rail.

For a week after the funeral I go into my own special kind of mourning: seeing nobody, never leaving the apartment or answering phone calls, eating little and drinking too much, but mostly just sleeping or watching television while crying and lying in bed. Then I turn the television off, answer every phone call, run along the river for twice as many miles than I usually do, go out for a big restaurant dinner with a friend and return to my job.

The Saturday morning after the next Saturday after that I sit on the bench near the place on the subway platform where Eliot was thrown off. I stay there from eight to around one, on the lookout for the two young men. I figure they live in the neighborhood and maybe every Saturday have a job or something to go to downtown and after a few weeks they'll think everything's forgotten about them and their crime and they can go safely back to their old routines, like riding the subway to work at the station nearest their homes. The descriptions I have of them are the ones the elderly witness gave. He said he was a portrait painter or used to be and so he was absolutely exact about their height, age, looks, mannerisms and hair color and style and clothes. He also made detailed drawings of the men for the police, which I have copies of from the newspaper, and which so far haven't done the police any good in finding them.

What I'm really looking out for besides those descriptions are two young men who will try and pick up or seriously annoy or molest a teen-age girl on the platform or do that to any reasonably young woman, including me. If I see them and I'm sure it's them I'll summon a transit policeman to arrest them and if there's none around then I'll follow the young men, though discreetly, till I see a policeman. And if they try and molest or terrorize me on the bench and no policeman's around, I'll scream at the top of my lungs till someone comes and steps in, and hopefully a policeman. But I just want those two young men caught, that's all, and am willing to risk myself a little for it, and though there's probably not much chance of it happening, I still want to give it a good try.

I do this every Saturday morning for months. I see occasional violence on the platform, like a man slapping his woman friend in the face or a mother hitting her infant real hard, but nothing like two or even one man of any description close to those young men terrorizing or molesting a woman or girl or even trying to pick one up. I do see men, both old and young, and a few who look no more than nine years old or ten, leer at women plenty as if they'd like to pick them up or molest them. Some men, after staring at a woman from a distance, then walk near to her when the train comes just to follow her through the same door into the car. But that's as far as it goes on the platform. Maybe when they both get in the car and especially when it's crowded, something worse happens. I know that a few times a year when I ride the subway, a pull or poke from a man has happened to me.

A few times a man has come over to the bench and once even a woman who looked manly and tried to talk to me, but I brushed them off with silence or a remark. Then one morning a man walks over when I'm alone on the bench and nobody else is around. I'm not worried, since he has a nice face and is decently dressed and I've seen him before here waiting for the train and all it seems he wants now is to sit down. He's a big man, so I move over a few inches to the far end of the bench to give him more room.

"No," he says, "I don't want to sit—I'm just curious. I've seen you in this exact place almost every Saturday for the last couple of months and never once saw you get on the train. Would it be too rude—"

"Yes."

"All right. I won't ask it. I'm sorry."

"No, go on, ask it. What is it you want to know? Why I sit here? Well I've been here every Saturday for more than three months straight, if you're so curious to know, and why you don't see me get on the car is none of your business, okay?"

"Sure," he says, not really offended or embarrassed. "I asked for and got it and should be satisfied. Excuse me," and he walks away and stands near the edge of the platform, never turning around to me. When the local comes, he gets on it.

Maybe I shouldn't have been that sharp with him, but I don't like to be spoken to by men I don't know, especially in subways.

Next Saturday around the same time he comes downstairs again and stops by my bench.

"Hello," he says.

I don't say anything and look the other way.

"Still none of my business why you sit here every Saturday like this?"

I continue to look the other way.

"I should take a hint, right?"

"Do you think that's funny?"

"No."

"Then what do you want me to do, call a policeman?"

"Of course not. I'm sorry and I ... being stupid."

"Look, I wouldn't call a policeman. You seem okay. You want to be friendly or so it seems. You're curious besides, which is good. But to me it is solely my business and not yours why I sit here and don't want to talk to you and so forth and I don't know why you'd want to persist in it."

"I understand," and he walks away, stays with his back to me and gets on the train when it comes.

Next Saturday he walks down the stairs and stays near the platform edge about ten feet away reading a book. Then he turns to me and seems just about to say something and I don't know what I'm going to say in return, if anything, because he does seem polite and nice and intelligent and I actually looked forward a little to seeing and speaking civilly to him, when the train comes. He waves to me and gets on it. I lift my hand to wave back but quickly put it down. Why start?

Next Saturday he runs down the stairs to catch the train that's pulling in. He doesn't even look at me this time, so in a rush is he to get on the car. He gets past the doors just before they close and has his back to me when the train leaves. He must be late for someplace.

The next Saturday he comes down the stairs and walks over to me with two containers of coffee or tea while the train's pull-

ing in. He keeps walking to me while the train doors open, close, and the train goes. I look at the advertisement clock. He's about fifteen minutes earlier than usual.

"How do you like your coffee if I can ask, black or regular? Or maybe you don't want any from me, if you do drink coffee, which would of course be all right too."

"Regular, but I don't want any, thanks."

"Come on, take it, it's not toxic and I can drink my coffee any old way. And it'll perk you up, not that you need perking up and certainly not from me," and he gives me a container. "Sugar?" and I say "Really, this is—" and he says "Come on: sugar?" and I nod and he pulls out of his jacket pocket a couple of sugar packets and a stirring stick. "I just took these on the way out of the shop without waiting for a bag, don't ask me why. The stick's probably a bit dirty, do you mind?" and I shake my head and wipe the stick though there's nothing on it. "Mind if I sit and have my coffee also?" and I say "Go ahead. It's not my bench and all that and I'd be afraid to think what you'd pull out of your pocket if I said no—probably your own bench and cock- tail table," and he says "Don't be silly," and sits.

He starts talking about the bench, how the same oak one has been here for at least thirty years because that's how long he's lived in the neighborhood, then about the coffee, that it's good though always from the shop upstairs a little bitter, then why he happens to see me every Saturday: that he's recently divorced and has a child by that marriage who he goes to in Brooklyn once a week to spend the whole day with. He seems even nicer and more intelligent than I thought and comfortable to be with and for the first time I think he's maybe even good- looking when before I thought his ears stuck out too far and he had too thin a mouth and small a nose. He dresses well anyway and has a nice profile and his hair's stylish and neat and his face shaven clean which I like and no excessive jewelry or neck chain which I don't and in his other jacket pocket are a paper- back and small ribbon-wrapped package, the last I guess a pres- ent for his little girl.

His train comes and when the doors open I say "Shouldn't you get on it?" and he says "I'll take the next one if you don't mind," and I say "I don't think it's up to me to decide," and he hunches his shoulders and gives me that expression "Well I don't know what to say," and the train goes and when it's quiet again he continues the conversation, now about what I think of something that happened in Africa yesterday which he read in the paper today. I tell him I didn't read it and that maybe when I do read my paper it won't be the same as his and so might not have that news story and he says "What paper you read?" and I tell him and he says "Same one—front page, left-hand column," and I say "Anyway, on Saturdays I don't, and for my own reasons, have time for the newspaper till I get home later and really also don't have the time to just sit here and talk," and he says "Of course, of course," but seriously, as if he believes me, and we're silent for a while, drinking our coffees and looking at the tracks.

We hear another train coming and I say "I think you better get on this one," and he says "Okay. It's been great and I hope I haven't been too much of a nuisance," and I say "You really haven't at all," and he says "Mind if I ask your name?" and I say "Your train," and he yells to the people going into the subway car "Hold the door," and gets up and says to me "Mine's Vaughn," and shakes my hand and says "Next week," and runs to the train with his container and he's not past the door a second when the man who kept it open for him lets it close.

I picture him on his way to Brooklyn, reading his book, later in Prospect Park with his daughter as he said they would do if the good weather holds up and in an indoor ice-skating rink if it doesn't, and then go back to my lookout. People spit and throw trash on the tracks, a drunk or crazy man urinates on the platform, a boy defaces the tile wall with a marker pen and tells me to go shoot myself when I very politely suggest he stop, there's almost a fight between a man trying to get off the train and the one blocking his way who's trying to get on, which I doubt would have happened if both sides of the double door had opened, but again no sign of my two young men.

Vaughn's not there the next Saturday and the Saturday after that and the third Saturday he's not there I begin thinking that I'm thinking more about him than I do of anybody or thing and spending more time looking at the staircase and around the platform for him than I do for those young men. I've gradually lost interest in finding them and over the last four months my chances

have gotten worse and worse that I'll even recognize them if they
ever do come down here and as far as their repeating that ha-
rassing-the-girl incident at this particular station, well forget it,
and I leave the station at noon instead of around my usual two
and decide that was my last Saturday there.

A month later I meet Vaughn coming out of a supermarket
when I'm going in. He's pulling a shopping cart filled with clean
laundry at the bottom and two big grocery bags on top. It's Saturday, we're both dressed in T-shirts and shorts for the warm
weather now, and I stop him by saying "Vaughn, how are you?"
He looks at me as if he doesn't remember me. "Maybe because
you can't place me anywhere else but on a subway bench. Maria
Pierce. From the subway station over there."

"That's right. Suddenly your face was familiar, but you never
gave me your name. What's been happening?" and I say "Nothing
much I guess," and he says "You don't wait in subway stations
anymore for whatever you were waiting for those days?" and I
say "How would you know? You stopped coming yourself there
and to tell you the truth I was sort of looking forward to a
continuation of that nice chat we last had."

"Oh, let me tell you what went wrong. My ex-wife, giving me
a day's notice, changed jobs and locations and took my daughter
to Boston with her. I could have fought it, but don't like arguments. I only get to see her when I get up there, which hasn't
happened yet, and maybe for August if I want."

"That's too bad. I remember how devoted you were."

"I don't know it's so bad. I'm beginning to enjoy my freedom
every Saturday, as much as I miss my kid. But I got to go. Ice
cream in the bag will soon be melting," and he says goodbye and
goes.

If I knew his last name I might look him up in the phone
book and call him and say something like "Since we live in the
same neighborhood, would you care to have a cup of coffee one
of these days? I owe you one and I'll even, if you're still curious,
let you in on my big secret why I every Saturday for months
waited at our favorite subway station." Then I think no, even if
I did have his phone number. I gave him on the street a couple
of openings to make overtures about seeing me again and he

didn't take them because he didn't want to or whatever his reasons but certainly not because of his melting ice cream.

Several weeks later I read in the newspaper that those two young men got caught. They were in the Eighth Street subway station and tried to molest a policewoman dressed like an artist with even a sketchbook and drawing pen, and two plain-clothesmen were waiting nearby. The police connected them up with Eliot's death. The two men later admitted to being on my subway platform that day but said they only started a fight with him because he tried to stop one of them from making a date with a girl the young man once knew. They said they told Eliot to mind his business, he refused, so they wrestled him to the ground and then said he could get up if he didn't make any more trouble. Eliot said okay, got up and immediately swung at them, missed, lost his footing and before either of them could grab him away, fell to the tracks. They got scared and ran to the street. They don't know the girl's last name or where she lives except that it's somewhere in the Bronx.

I buy all the newspapers that day and the next. One of them has a photo of the young men sticking their middle fingers up to the news photographers. They don't look anything like the young men I was on the lookout for, so either the witness's description of them or the printing of the photograph was bad, because I don't see how they could have physically changed so much in just a few months.

I continue to read the papers for weeks after that, hoping to find something about the young men going to trial, but don't. Then a month later a co-worker of mine who knew about Eliot and me says she saw on the television last night that the young men were allowed to plead guilty to a lesser charge of negligent manslaughter or something and got off with a jail term of from one to three years. "It seems the elderly man, that main witness to Eliot's murder, died of a fatal disease a while ago and the young woman witness could never be found. As for molesting the policewoman, that charge was dropped, though the news reporter never said why."

ON THE BEACH

Eva, Olivia and Eric are on a beach trying to drag a rowboat into the water. "This thing will never budge," Eric says. "My father could make it budge," Eva says. "Here she goes again," Olivia says. "No, let her, what?" Eric says. "My father was so strong he could lift it on his back and carry it into the water. He'd need both arms and it'd be heavy but he could do it." "I'm sure he could. Or push, even, or at least drag it into the water by himself, but I can't, honey. I'm simply not as strong as your father was." "As my father is. My father's very strong." "As he is then. As you say. I've heard of his physical exploits—how strong he was, I'm saying." "She knows what exploits are," Olivia says. "You don't have to teach it to either of us. I know the word and I've told her the word." "I didn't realize that. For you see, I didn't know that word till I was twice your age, maybe three times. How old are you? I'm only kidding. I know how old. I even know how old both of you are put together. A hundred six, right. No. But good for you—both of you for knowing so many big impressive words. Like 'impressive.' You know that word too, right?" "Right." "Sure, just as my father knows all those words and more," Eva says. "He knows words that haven't even been born yet. Like kakaba. Like oolemagoog." "He does? He knows those? Wow. Very impressive. Anyway, I'd hoped we got past that subject. I said that to myself. But if we didn't, some men are just stronger than others. That's a fact. I'd be the last to deny it. You both know what 'deny' means, I know. And some men are smarter than others. And kinder and nicer than others and have more hair and so on. But I bet no man has more than two arms. Anyone want to bet?" "My father's stronger, nicer, kinder than others and much much more than that," Eva says. "He's taller than most others. And handsome. Much more than any others. His photos say so. Others say so." "Well that's a good thing for a man to be," Eric says. "For an older woman to be too," Olivia says. "That's what Mother says." "Good. She knows. She's smart. Me, I was never considered handsome. That should come as no surprise to you two, as it doesn't to your mother. Not handsome even when I was a young man, an older woman, a small piggy, or even now as a fairly not-so-young-maybe-even-old hog. Most of that was supposed to be funny. Why aren't you laughing?" "Because it wasn't funny and we're talking about someone else now, right, Olivia?" "I don't know," Eva says. "Daddy. All that he is." "Okay," Eric says, "I'll bite. Meaning, well, just that I'm all pointy ears and curly tail uncoiled and extended snout—I want to know. What else was he? *Is* he. Sorry. But tell me." "Funny," Eva says. "He's more funny than anyone alive. Sometimes people died laughing at things he said. But really, with big holes in their chests and all their bones broken and blood." "Yes, that's true," Olivia says, "the streets covered with broken laughed-out dead bodies, for funniest is what he is and always was. And liveliest too. A real live wire, our father. You're excellent, Eric—honestly, this is not to go stroke-stroke to you. And lively and smart, but not at all hand-some, and kind and wonderful in some ways and we love you, we truly do, even if what Eva said and how she acted just now, but you're not livelier than our dad. No sir. Our real dad was *live*-ly! Oh boy was he. A real live wire. He was also so sad. We shouldn't leave that out if we want to be fair. A real sad wire. 'Mr. Sad Wire' we should've called him, right, Eva? If you could have talked then. For you couldn't even say three words in a row that made sense. No sentence-sense I used to say about her then, Eric." "I could so say sad wire." "Hey, stop a moment, for where are we?" Eric says. "Was? Is? Which one is he?" "Is," Eva says. "Daddy's definitely an 'is.' And sometimes when I hear from him, like I did just yesterday, I say 'Daddy Live Wire, Daddy Sad Wire, how dost your farting grow?' Because that's what he also does best—just ask Olivia." "That's right, she's a true bird, we have to be fair," Olivia says. "He was probably the world's greatest most productive farter for more years in a row than anybody and still is." "Is for sure," Eva says. "The whole world knows of him. He's been in newspapers, on TV. People have died from it everywhere, and not happy laughing deaths. In planes and parks. Hundreds of dead bodies in your way sometimes. Flat on the ground, piled ten deep sometimes, black tongues hanging out, their own hands around their necks. Vultures in trees all around but refusing to pick at them the smell's so bad. And much worse. I won't even go into it more. Like whole cities dying, dogs and cats too—not a single breathing thing left alive. Maybe that's an exaggeration. Rats always survive. But 'Killer Dad's been at it again,' I always say to Olivia when we see this, and that time we walked through that ghost city. It doesn't hurt us because we got natural, natural . . . what is it again we got, Olivia?" "Impunity. Immunity. Ingenuity. That's us. We never even smell it when we're in the midst of it but we can see when we see all this that it can only be he who did it." "You girls are really funny today," Eric says. "Inherited from him, no doubt." "Oh no we didn't," Olivia says. "He inherited it from us, didn't you know? Something strange happened in life when we were born. But everything he's best at he got from us, or almost. We're sad live wires or lively dad wires or just mad love wires. That's because we brought up our father and are still doing it yet. Now that's a real switch, isn't it, Eva, bringing up your own dad? How'd we do it?" "I'm not sure, but that's for sure what we're doing. We didn't want to, we had our own lives to bring up, but we had no choice, right, Olivia?" "No, why?" "No, you." "He was left on our doorstep, right? Came in a shoe box with a note glued to it saying . . . what?" "It said 'Feeling blue? Nothing in life's true? Cat's got your goo? So do something different in your loo today. Bring up your own dad. But don't leave him in a shoe box for squirrels to build their nests in on top of him. Take him out, brush him off, give him a good cleaning. Treat him as good as you would your best pair of party shoes.' Wasn't that what it said, Olivia?" "Or was it a hat box he came in? 'Put him on your bean against the sun, sleet and rain and your brain will seem much keener.' No, that wasn't it. 'Treat him as gently as you would your own mentally . . . ' I forget everything it said. But we did. And I know it was some kind of box." "A suggestion box. A lunch box. 'What's inside is nutritious and suspicious. Open hungrily and with care.' And when we've brought him up all the way, Eric, I'm afraid the sad news is you'll have to move out. Because he'll be moving back in, all grown up then. Because no bigamists allowed in our family, right, Olivia?" "Right, Eva." "So?" "So maybe in yours, Eric, it's allowed, but not in ours. Family honor. Horses' code. New York telephone directory. We're very sorry. Unbreakable rule. But let's stop, Eva. I've spun out and so have you. And we're not being nice to Eric who's been so nice to us. Renting this boat. Helping us push it into the water. Doing most of the work. Probably getting a heart attack from it. Dying for us just so we can have some summer fun." "Hey, don't worry about me, kids. Let it out. Have it out. Thrash it to me. Money and abuse are no object. Listen, I know how you're both feeling, but you have to know I also of course wish he had never died." "He never did, how can you say that?" Eva says. "Whatever. And easy as it is for me to say this after the fact and much as I would have missed if he had lived—I'll be straightforward with you— I didn't know him but have heard so many wonderful things about him that I only wish I had." "Had what?" Olivia says. "That he can't be replaced. By me. I know that. Never deluded myself otherwise. And that I wish I'd known him." "So, it can be arranged," Eva says, "can't it, Olivia?" "Let's stop—really. We're spoiling our day and being extra extra lousy to Eric." "Okay, he's dead, heave-ho, hi-heave, what d'ya say, Joe, bury the problem? For what I want most now is to get out there to fish, splash and row." "Well," Eric says, "it seems we'll have to wait for a couple of strapping guys to come along and help us or come back when the tide comes in. Anyone think to bring that card with the tide times?" "Daddy will come help," Eva says. "Sometimes it only takes one and he's the one. So hey, hi, daddy of mine, come and pull our boat into the water. You'll see. I've wished. Daddy come now," and she sits down hard in the sand, puts her thumb in her mouth and sucks it while she twiddles her hair in back and looks off distantly. "Eva, get up, get up quickly, you hear me?" Olivia says. "You're scaring the shit out of us."

THE TRUE STORY

I'm walking past a cheap Village hotel. It's on a side street. I didn't know it was cheap, but later I do, and a woman comes out of it, taller than I, much younger too, long heavy fur coat that looks worn and old and she says from a couple of yards away while she's approaching me "Would you like me to be your date tonight?"

"What?"

"You didn't actually hear me?"

"Only something about a date."

"Would you like me to be your date tonight?"

"I really would but I'm going to a party now."

"Oh well," and she walks away.

I continue in the direction I was heading and then turn around. She's near the corner, opening her handbag. I run to her. She turns around quickly as if expecting trouble.

"Oh," she says. "What do you want?"

"Would you like to come to the party?"

"Thanks but no."

"Why not?"

"I won't know anyone there."

"You'll know me by the time we get there."

"No, I don't think so."

"You don't think you'll know me? We could stop in a bar first for a drink."

"Drink sounds okay but when I said no I don't think so I

meant I didn't think I want to go to the party even if I knew you. I don't like going to strange places with lots of strangers around. And my clothes aren't nice. Really."

"Your clothes are fine. Look at mine. It's just my coat that's nice." I open my coat and show her my clothes. "And there won't be many people. They're all very pleasant, mostly friends."

"I still won't know any of them and they won't appreciate me. They'll say to you where'd you find me."

"I'll tell them 'One hour ago outside this hotel.'"

"Thanks loads."

"Why, what's wrong? You were lonely, that's what I'll say. Or not that, that's no good, but they know I'm single, so something that we'll say happened to you like you just had a fight with your husband—"

"I have no husband."

"I'm just making that up. Your husband or boyfriend or even your mother—for the story we'll give these people at the party."

"I don't want to give anybody any story."

"But say you did come with me."

"I won't."

"But say you did."

"Listen, it's cold. I was about to phone someone, but you want to have a drink?"

"Sure. There's a bar I know over there."

We walk to it. It's on Sixth Avenue. I say "So let's say you came with me and I tell them you had a fight with your best friend or anyone like that and you were anxious to talk to someone about it or some serious problem you had and you saw me and it suddenly occurred to you then or maybe even when you were riding down the elevator of the hotel—"

"It has no elevator."

"How will these people know?"

"They might ask what hotel and if I say which one they'll know I'm lying because one of them could know that hotel and it has no elevator."

"Okay. Let's get our stories straight for them if we do go to the party."

"I'm not, but okay, let's get the story straight. You're buying the drinks so you have the right to tell stories."

"No more right than you have no matter who's buying. You can tell one if you like and as long as you want it to be."

"I don't know any and I don't like to."

"Let's just go in and order and we'll talk some more."

We go into the bar. I ask what she wants. She says scotch and soda. I order a glass of wine for me. Bartender gives the two drinks to us, I pay and we sit at a table in back. "Okay. Where were we?" I say.

"To your health."

"To our health. Of course." We click glasses and drink. "All right. You came out of the hotel without an elevator. The hotel had no elevator. We got that far. But while you were in the hotel in your room, we'll say, you had a bad fight with your best friend—a male, who was up there chatting or dropping something off for you and you said to yourself right after he left 'The hell with that guy. I'm going downstairs and make a date with the first decently dressed and seeming man that comes along, just to show him and also to have a good time.'"

"That never happened."

"Say it did, that's all I'm asking—I'm no psychic. You just had that quick-as-a-moment thought in your room. You wanted to teach that other man a lesson or do something wild tonight like ask a stranger for a date. Nothing's wrong with that. If a man can do it, why not you? And people can understand that impulse or frivolousness and probably most have wanted to do it in the same circumstances too but never had the courage. And you did ask me."

"I asked if you wanted me to be your date. You don't know what that means?"

"I'm sure I do but maybe I don't completely. What does it mean, just in case I don't?"

"First tell me what you think it does."

"That you wanted us to have a drink and talk and you'll tell me your story, even if you say you don't have one—why you asked to be my date and so on. And I'll tell you mine or several and that'll be after a couple of drinks and we'll know something about one another by then and maybe later we'll go to a movie or for dinner and I'll walk you home and say good night and get your phone number if you don't mind or I'll come in and say good night till the morning when I'll say good morning—you know what I mean. In other words it could end up with our possible sleeping together through the night. Or you might even end up at my place."

"You have a place alone near here?"

"Yes."

"Then we can go to your place if it's not a mile-high climb upstairs. I don't like my hotel. Too shabby, dirty, they don't clean and it's noisy, walls like thread. And no movies, dinner. No boyfriend, best male friend, husband, mother—none of that. I just occasionally need money. So when I do I go downstairs or wherever, if I'm out of a job and can't borrow, and ask a man who's alone and dressed well but isn't too young and doesn't look like a cop and also like he can afford it if he wants me to be his date. If he says yes, we talk. Sometimes in a bar, sometimes right on the street where I meet him, but discreetly. He asks how much, I tell him. We don't bargain. If he still wants me to be his date, we go to my hotel if we have to, because I don't want them getting ideas there that meeting men is all I do, so better to his place if he seems okay and has one alone and nearby and doesn't mind my coming up or to another nearby hotel if he can pay for it. You have that clear now?"

"Yes."

"I only do this when I absolutely have to and with the men I've picked I've never been wrong."

"They've always said yes?"

"No, but the ones who did always were polite and generous."

"I see now."

"Then you surely don't want me to come to your party."

"Yes, I still do. I do."

"Why would you? That's so crazy. Besides, you'd be wasting my time. One date for me tonight isn't going to pay my back build-up of rent and the food bill, which is what I need tonight, mine and the cat's, besides next week's too."

"How much would you make—maybe I shouldn't ask you this."

"Just ask. We're being honest and free and if it's something I have to hide, I'll let you know."

"How much if you had the number of dates you think you would get tonight?"

"Hundred fifty."

"I don't have that. I couldn't spare it even if I did. I've twenty-five and change on me."

"Twenty-five will be all right. How close you live nearby?"

"I'm going to a party. I don't want to go back to my home with you right now or your hotel room and maybe not even later. I want to go to the party and I want to take you and I'll give you the twenty-five to come along. You won't meet men there and I wouldn't want you to for the purposes you might want. I mean, well maybe you might meet men—how do I know what can happen and you're attractive and in the end that's your concern what arrangements you make with men, and if all that came out sounding nasty or cynical what I said or any of it, I didn't intend it that way. Now do you want to come with me or not?"

"No. But answer me one thing before I leave here. If you don't want me to be your date for that twenty minutes and however many it takes to get to your place, which I don't think you do, how come you want to take me to your party and give me twenty-five dollars for going to it—it just doesn't make sense."

"The twenty-five's to help you with your bills. It's probably enough to put off your creditors for a day and I don't expect anyone to make immediate complete sacrifices for me, one hundred percent and so forth, when their other worries or concerns go way beyond anything dealing with me. As for the rest of your question, at first I did think you weren't what you said you only occasionally are, or not that, but at least wanted me to do with you what I at first didn't think you wanted me to. Maybe that doesn't make much language sense or something but I did at first think you were lonely and wanted a date tonight in the sense of date—to have a meeting or appointment for one between two people for the mutual enjoyment of some kind of social activity but not necessarily sex. So I thought, why not? I thought that then. You seemed pleasant and now intelligent. You're attractive as I said. And definitely frank and loose in the sense of being open with your thoughts, far as I can tell, and what you feel, besides your vivacity and enthusiasm, all of which I like too, but not all of which was I able to gauge so quickly when I first met you. And I don't have a date tonight and just about everyone at the party will—a companion they came with, husbands and wives, men and women friends, all-to-mostly coupled. I might even be the only truly single person there, not that it bothered me till maybe when I began thinking of it with you. Secondly, now that I know what you wanted to have a date for—but I'm not answering this correctly or whatever, am I?"

"You're not answering it just about at all. All I asked was why you still want to take me there. It can't be because you might be the only single."

"No. I also wanted to continue talking to you because I think what you'd have to say over one evening when we were socializing rather than in the thirty-minute span when we were just biff-banging and walking to and from the place of sex, would be very interesting—more interesting than my going alone to the party, though even more interesting if we were both at the party. No, that still doesn't sound clear or right. Maybe, almost probably certainly, because after the party you might also consent to coming to my apartment and then I would have the best of both evenings—party and now this, when we could make love. Because then I wouldn't have to pay for it, which I don't like doing, and it would be better because we could take our time, there'd be no thought that a man just preceded me—that and maybe you'd even be grateful that I took you to someplace nice and you had a good time among friendly people but something that was maybe untypical in your experiences—but that must sound so self-serving and egotistical, it does to me."

"I've been to lots of nice parties before. I go to them as often as almost anyone and ones without pressures too."

"Of course. But that's all. Just that we'd go together and you'd talk, I'd talk, together, to other people, you might have to lie a little, I don't know. I'd have to lie a little about you too. Or we could both lie about the same thing: we met on the street, you were lonely, etcetera—that story about coming out of the hotel which doesn't have an elevator, etcetera. Or you could have been upset because your dog or cat jumped out of your window and you were upstairs when it happened but downstairs when I met you—the ambulance had just taken the dead animal away, or injured if you don't like it dead. And I was passing by on my way to the party and asked or you asked if I could talk to you because you were so heartbroken and lived alone or your roommate was out of town or away for the night and I bought you a drink for your nerves and we talked at the bar or restaurant and that's when I invited you to the party, more to take your mind off the cat—something like that. And we'd eat the good party spread they'd have there, maybe drink too much, and if you wanted to smoke I'm sure there'll be some people there who smoke and will let you join their circle—I don't like to but you just go ahead. And then when most of the guests have left or are leaving I'll get our coats and we'll leave too and cab to my apartment—that is, only if you want to. And I won't try anything funny with you—meaning I'm not a masher or beater or anything weird. That I'm not. We might have a nightcap. You might want to change your mind at my place and leave. Or you could even take a shower if you like. No pressures about any of those either. Do what you want. I won't leap into the shower or tub with you and insist you scrub my back. And then I'll light the fireplace and we could sit in front of it—I'm not kidding, I actually have one and plenty of kindling and hard wood and you could undress me if we haven't already undressed and I'll undress you or we'll undress separately if we undress at all—"

"Can I have another drink?"

"Sure. I'll get it."

I go to the bar and get another scotch and glass of wine and bring them back.

"Where was I? We were in front of the fireplace?"

"I was thinking," she says.

"Yes?"

"Let's go to the party. We'll stick with the lie you just made up. I like the cat out the window. That sounds real because it sounds possible and I do have one in my room so I know how they love ledges and what they're like if anyone asks me about him and the stupid things he can do. And you made the party sound like fun—the whole evening. I won't let myself meet anyone else and I'll leave when you want us to or maybe a little before then when I want to if I'm feeling uncomfortable there or things get sticky. You've been nice and I expect you to stay nice. But you can't kick me out of your apartment at three or four in the morning, all right?"

"Why would I?"

"Some guys have. Even the ones I was in love with. Suddenly

they don't want me. Maybe I can't blame them sometimes—the new ones I just meet overnight. They get scared their wife or girlfriend's coming home or that's just an excuse and they want me out because they've had enough of me or they suddenly feel guilty or even diseased sleeping with me. Or listen to this, they have to go to work extra early that morning they say and don't want me in their apartment alone. I don't want you doing that."

"Tomorrow's Sunday. I've the weekend off. If you come to my apartment—though who knows what could happen by then. I might get drunk at the party, though I don't usually, and make a stupid scene about something else and you'll get embarrassed or frightened and leave without me and regret you ever met me."

"You won't do that?"

"No. What I'm saying is anything can happen to spoil it but I doubt very seriously anything will. We'll go to the party and stick with the story. We'll talk, eat, drink, leave around the same time everyone else does, cab to my apartment if you still want to and light a fire and take a shower or anything like that but all reasonable, sane, comfortable, etcetera. Then we'll go to bed or even make love on the rug in front of the fire or wait till morning for that or not even in the morning—not ever—anything you want."

"And you'll give me twenty-five more dollars when we get to your place?"

"That I can't do."

"You have no more money at home?"

"I have but I don't want to give it."

"But I need at least fifty to keep the landlady away. And I'm already sacrificing a lot by going to the party for just that single twenty-five. The other men. Those are the best hours of the best day of the week for that. By one o'clock I could make one-fifty if I work real hard and am lucky—a hundred at the very least."

"I can't give you anything but the twenty-five I'll give now if you come to the party with me. It just wouldn't be the same thing giving you more at home."

"Then I can't go."

"Be reasonable. One evening."

"No I can't."

"Then don't."

"I won't."

She finishes her drink says goodbye and leaves. I go to the party and meet someone new and just as the party's ending I ask and she says yes and we cab to my apartment.

CAPITAL LABOR

A friend of my sister calls and says "I was chatting with Lula just before and asked how you are and she said looking for work and I said 'Yeah? Because something's come up in our real estate office he might be interested in, think I should call him?' and she said 'I don't think so because Mort hates any kind of stuffy office work,' and I said 'But it's mostly outside in the sun among the birds and city trees,' and she said 'He still hates any kind of hard-core money-making work including artistic, but chance it and call him because this time who knows?' So I'm calling. You think you'd mind working for us full-time for a month if I tell you what it is?"

"I'd like some steady work after going through two jobs in a week."

"Wonderful. We want someone to act as our rental agent for five recently renovated buildings in the Eighties on the West Side. They're all close together so no hardship for you to get to, one from the other not a block apart. What you have to do is hang around the buildings and sometimes in the office in one of the vacant apartments where there's a phone. So if people see our To Let signs on the buildings if you can't grab the more inter-ested-looking prospectives off the street—you'll get the knack quick—they'll call and you can be right down and around the corner or wherever to show them around. No pay. But one-third the rental fee if you rent the apartment. If the tenant refuses to pay the fee, since they might be wise we also own the building we're acting as agents for, then fifty dollars for each apartment you rent and ten dollars more for a two- instead of a one-year lease. September's the key month for renting, so you can clear a thousand minimum for a few weeks work and probably earn more. Sound okay?"

I go to her office. It's in the old General Motors building, top floor. The furniture looks like wood but is formica, the bright orange carpet clashes with the dark furniture and walls. The reception room's unkempt: trash cans spilling over, ashtrays smelly and full, boxes of photocopy-machine paper on the chairs and couches, empty matchbooks and squashed soda straws on the floor. But the walls and pilasters are made of real oak from the old days and with decorations in the coffered ceiling around where the chandeliers must have hung looking like something out of a French château or New York turn-of-the-century townhouse.

"Meet Larry, my boss," Penny says.

We go into his office. Larry's sitting in a big chair behind a wide desk with his back to me but swivels around and puts some legal papers down and we shake hands. He's about my age. "So sit down, sit down," he says. "Like some coffee?"

"No thanks."

"It's from a Mr. Coffee maker and special Jamaican blend. No sweat in making it."

"Had a cup before I came."

"It also makes hot water for tea."

"Leave him alone," Penny says. "He doesn't feel thirsty, don't bug him."

"Who's bugging? I'm being polite."

"I don't want any, thanks," I say. "Nice place you have here. Looks like where the GM chairman of the board himself might have worked."

"Hey man, very close. This suite was for their president. It's the penthouse. Where I sit is where he did. Let me show you his slide-away bar." He presses a button under his desk and two cabinet doors open and a bar appears. "The liquor didn't come with it. Like a drink?"

"Too early."

"Good for you. You passed my only test. Too early for me also and I don't want to employ a lush, especially for out there."

"Sneaky," Penny says.

"Why? I got rid of that other guy what's his name, Pigmigansky—"

"Parmiagiano."

"Parmesan cheese, okay, but I got rid of him the same way, didn't I? And later we heard he was a lush and a half. Same job as yours he applied for, Mort, and nobody ever looked more refined on so little dough. Too bad too. He knew his stuff. Psyched this suite out immediately as the finest he's ever seen and knew all the names of the architect styles: New Renaissance, Neo-Smorgasbord. He said we have the best view in New York. You ever seen one like it?"

"Something like it. When I was in a paying play once, I went to a dentist on Central Park South to have a couple of teeth capped."

"It couldn't've been anything like this. Here, take a look from this window. There's the lake. Way back there's Harlem. What are those twin towers off 110th? They really sunk a bundle into those beauties and are going to lose most of their teeth. You see, we're all attorneys here, Mrs. Rothblatt excluded—"

"Penny," Penny says.

"Penny. You know each other. And we're in lots of different businesses here, so I thought this suite and the park and Queens and Brooklyn and all the bridges at their feet would impress our clients, and it works. Everything in life is show, right?"

"I don't know."

"What're you talking about? You're an actor Penny says. You said it yourself about your capped teeth. So you most of anybody knows from shows and clothes and the impression you make is the impression people keep. Maybe now you can't afford that kind of show. 'Between jobs' you people like to say, which is why you're here and we get the benefit from it—but with us, more scratch we put out for show, more we get back, but proportionately. Same with any effort except sex sometimes and sitting on the toilet, present feminine company excluded."

"Mort knows. Women don't go potty. Tell him what he came here for."

He tells me about my job, hours and duties. "More time you work at it, more money you make and quicker you get your commissions from us. One September we had a guy who practically slept on the street to rent our apartments and he rented all of them in a week what would have taken anyone else a month. A real hustler. Remember Gatbar?"

"Gainsborough. He's in jail now," Penny says.

"Not for anything he did for us. He was a clean Gene all the way, not a light bulb was missing. Did I cover everything, Pen?"

"You better show Mort the apartments so he knows what he's selling and where his office is at."

"Where's the keys, Mrs. Rothbrains?"

She takes them out of her purse, a ring of about two hundred keys.

"We haven't got them all marked yet," he says, "but the super's going to do that today."

"Marked yet? That's a laugh."

"Everything to her's a laugh. I ought to get you replaced with a TV laugh track. You know, can you for canned laughter. Hey, to me that's funny, no?"

"Wonderful. I showed a prospective an apartment today but actually couldn't because after going through the ninety-ninth key that didn't fit the front door, she left. Can you blame her? You got to get each door key marked or you're going to rent zero this year."

"That's what I said. Joe the super. I guess we can take a cab over. Think I can be back for the Danube case by four?"

"It shouldn't take you any longer than that," Penny says. "Mail these on the way?" She gives him a packet.

"I'm paying her but she acts like my boss. Hey, you pay me from your salary from now on, all right?"

"Great, if you triple mine."

"A raise? I'll give you a raise. Sure I'll give you, a triple one. And next week I get to play the boss. Alternate weeks, got it?"

"Wonderful. Don't get lost."

We get a cab. In it he says "You know, I also was an actor once. Not seriously for the movies like you maybe, but commercials. I'm married but was seeing this actress, an unbelievable beauty. Boobs out to here and waist my thumb and middle finger went around and I'm stubby. I won't mention her name because she's right on top and making a million now and might not like it because acting people can gossip, I know that. I've seen you guys on panel shows. But at one party we're at there's a television ad man who says to me am I an actor or model? I said 'Me, you kidding?' and he said it's because I might look like one. That I have just the right face they need, rough and ugly, and would I like to audition for a shampoo ad. I asked if it pays and he said 'plenty.' 'Then you've hired me, baby,' and I took this film test and the ad got the okay from the soap company and was seen network to network twenty times a night for I don't know how many months and I'm still getting residuals from it, three years later. They still put it on. Same product but a little changed with an XYZ formula now in it, but still with me sudsing my hair like King Kong. Gave me enough to live on for two years if my expenses weren't so irrationally high. You like money?"

"I need it to live on. I like it all right."

"I love it, that's how much I like it. More than anything except the health you can't buy with it. But for the health care you can buy with it I love it for that reason also and everything else it buys. That's not original thinking, I know, but for me it's true. But why be original? Play in, I say, play in. But I respect you. I'm not kidding. You're a serious artist Penny says—an actor but artist, right? And I respect all serious people for what they do no matter how many years it takes them. Me, it has to come quick. That's why I'm both lawyer and in real estate and a businessman, but what I'm most serious and do best at is being a baker. Making bread. Bread: money. No? Hey, good thing my seriousness isn't in selling jokes."

We stop in front of one of his buildings. He tries to get into the apartment that will also serve as my office till I rent it. After going through the entire key ring and some of the keys two and three times each and in both key positions and on both locks, he whacks the key ring against the knob and says "I'd kick the shit out of this door if it wasn't mine," and we go outside. Joe the super comes by on his bike.

"I'll get them all marked by tomorrow," Joe says.

"Tonight," Larry says. "Then get your ass out here early tomorrow morning to give my keys to Mort."

"Tonight. You bet. Meet me here at ten on the spot, Mort."

"Nine," Larry says.

"Nine. Good. I'll get them all etched in with my stamp machine I got. For instance, that one on your ring I can see is already 3B for number 57 down the block. So some of the keys will be no problem."

"How do you know it's 3B's?" Larry says.

"By the grooves and lock make. See, I got an exact one of each myself," and he jangles a ring of about two hundred keys on his belt. "Some are already marked of mine and the most aren't because I don't have to. I got those memorized by heart." He aligns a key on his ring with one of Larry's. They do look alike.

"Let's get in there then. I want to show Mort at least one apartment before we go."

Joe tries to get into 3B with Larry's key. It doesn't work. He tries his own. Goes in but doesn't turn.

"I was sure this was the right one. Maybe the last tenant changed the lock. That bum. Burglarized by his own friends he also steals from us everything from spigots and bathroom tiles. Junkies. That's why we got him out and the first-floor tenant's also vacant. Nobody wanted to live in the same building with him."

"Let's try that one," Larry says. "It's a duplex, our highest rental, and at least it's open."

The front door of 1B has no cylinder in it so Joe just pushes it open. The place is a mess. Holes in the plaster walls, some floor planks ripped out, a closet door hanging by a mangled hinge, the banister to the windowless playroom below, which makes it a duplex, lying on the stairs.

"Dwayne David had it last," Larry says.

"Who?" I say.

"The actor-performer, star of *The Magic Feet*. Real pothead. Built his own loft out of ropes and hammocks and puffed puffed puffed with his boy and girl cuties all day except on matinees. I don't see how you never heard of him, but use him as a strong selling point. People like to live where there were stars."

He shows me the garden which he says has 3B's garbage in it. "I'll have it cleaned out, but see the kind of slobs we get? That's what I want to change from now on. One thing I want to warn you about renting these places is if a dude pulls up in a new pimpmobile and wears a fancy pimp outfit and Superfly hat and says 'Hey daddy, jive, give me five,' and gives you the hand-slapping number for a greeting but on the application says he's a tailor, tailor him the hell out of here or tell him he hasn't a chance to get a mouse hole in this building because your boss doesn't let pimps in, understand? Don't be afraid of offending anyone."

"I don't see how I could say that."

"Then tell him his application will be processed summarily, but don't take a deposit as that one we just tear up. With the last pimp in 4A it was like a screaming slave market in there. He even threw a live dog out the window."

"We don't know if it was alive," Joe says.

"We even sure it was a dog? God, what pigs."

Larry and I go to Columbus Avenue for a taxi. As I'm stepping into the cab I tell him I've changed my mind and now want to walk home.

"I guess it's good for you, exercise. But one last thing. No renting to more than two black families per building, got it? No matter if they're all college presidents and the building has ten vacancies in it like number 7."

"I don't think I can do that either."

"All right. If it's against your principles, put an asterisk on the bottom right-hand corner of the application so I know the applicant's black. It's not against my principles. I don't like them. Neither do most of my tenants. They bring down the property value and destroy the building because they hate the landlord. Even the blacks I let in tell me to keep more out, so if you think you're doing anyone a favor, think about that."

I think about the asterisk that night and don't know what to do. I call a friend and ask her what she'd do in the same position and circumstances—"If you hadn't a hundred dollars to your name and could possibly make a thousand or two in a month."

Doris says "How would you explain carrying out the duties of this job to Max?" who's a mutual friend of ours and black.

"Is it necessary for me to tell him?"

"I'll tell him."

So I write my decision in a note to Larry, saying that "even putting that asterisk on the page presents moral problems to me," and at nine next morning show up at the meeting spot with the super to give him the note and application forms when he's supposed to give me the keys.

Joe comes at ten, says "Sorry, I got tangled up with a broad. Tenant who wanted her window puttied. Then quick, she's pulling off my pants if I can get Larry to forget her three months' back rent. Promise everything, give nothing, Larry says. I'll tell you her apartment when I'm tired of her or she finds out I can't help. What's this? Not taking the job? Go screw yourself then, for why I even bother? I had to fly down from heaven to this when I wasn't even done yet? I haven't the keys marked for you anyhow," and he pedals off.

That night Larry calls and says "You really wasted my time yesterday, but I want to tell you something more I hope you won't forget. Don't mention to anyone what our renting policy to blacks is. If ever one comes in haughty and confident to see their denied applications, which they're entitled by law to, but says they know what that asterisk means or whatever new little mark we put on it or some dude named Mort also told them about our renting policy and they're going to court to get in our building, I'm going to send a couple men over to talk some sense into your head. I mean that. That's how outraged I'll get if I have to let in one more black than I have to because of you."

I call Doris and say "I didn't take the job for the reasons you didn't want me to, but for my own sake keep what I told you about their not renting to blacks to yourself."

"I already told Max, just in conversation, and he said he was contacting a local anti-racist league."

I call Max and he says "If I'd have known your head depended on it I still would have told the league. These things have to be exposed. We all have to take chances sometimes—you as well as me. You call Larry back and tell him I told the league and if he's got any men to send over to send them to me and give him my address. And feel privileged you were put in the position to get that data, because none of us could. Anyhow, don't worry. Most of these Larrys make threats all day but are just big windbags and I'd sit tight and call his bluff."

I call Penny, tell her what's happened and ask if Larry's serious about sending men over to rough me up.

"Oh he's serious all right. He can be a real thug and knows who to go to to get what and now I'm afraid for your life. I never should have got you involved but didn't think you were bent that way."

"How can you work for him if he's like that?"

"It's a job when they're not too easy to find and you think mine's the only one where someone has to compromise? You should have made a couple compromises also if you wanted to work that bad and you now wouldn't be in such a spot. Besides, Larry's a damn nice guy outside of those things, pays a great wage, doesn't breathe down my neck about the pettiest things like my previous bosses did, gives me plenty of room and control and what he does that I have no part of or care for is his business and it also goes to keeping a dozen honest workers on the books and their families fed. Like our own government might kill or detain perfectly innocent people but we still pay our taxes and don't complain about these illegalities too much, true? But I think I have the solution for you. I'll tell Larry you blurted out something before you knew you shouldn't have and that to make amends you told your black friend and his league that you were lying about our renting practices, more to momentarily break up the seriousness of their cause a little and have a good laugh with him, but it backfired."

"He wouldn't believe me."

"Say you were lying anyway. Your friend will at least know you won't go into court on their behalf, and if he still won't listen to you, phone the league and tell them yourself."

"Why don't I just phone the police and tell them Larry's threatened me?"

"You have it on paper? Your sister's my best friend besides? And excuse me, but I tried to do you a favor and you now want to lose me my job that took a half-year to get? And what'll you do when the cops stop protecting you if they ever start? Don't come to me. Be smart. Drop the matter entirely and look elsewhere for your crusade."

I call Max and tell him I was told by Larry's office to say I was lying about its rental policies. "But what it really means is that I'm afraid of him and that whatever you told the league I said I'm going to say isn't so or was just drunk talk or something when I told you it."

"Then I'll call the league and tell them my friend was mistaken and they have no case. But about you and me, Mort, I don't see how I'll ever be able to see you again," and hangs up.

Doris calls later and says "For the first time since I've known you you can do something for people actively, not just verbally, and you give that up and Max's friendship just to protect yourself over some punk's probably baseless threat?"

"It wasn't baseless."

"They actually threatened your life?"

"They intimated."

"That isn't the same thing."

"Trying to find out if they'll go through with it could be. But I didn't want you to know and still don't because that could put you in danger too."

"I'm not worried about myself when it comes to this matter and certainly Max isn't worried about him, so why should you be about you?"

"I'm worried about Max and you."

"Just answer me."

"I'm worried about me, Max and you."

"That still doesn't answer it."

"I'm more involved with it than either of you, can't you see?"

"No, you've no guts. Nothing to back up your big principles. Hell with it. I've lost all my respect for you just as Max has," and hangs up.

I call back and say "Please understand what I'm up against, Doris," and she says "And you try and understand me. If I can't respect you, how can I still see you? Bye."

Next day Penny calls and says "How'd it work out?" and I tell her and she says she's sorry and tells me to hold on and she comes back to the phone and says "I just spoke to Larry and it's all right with him, if it is with you, since he feels you've nothing to lose now and he's already put the time in to show you how, to work for us at the same job if you adapt to our policy about those asterisks and things."

"I don't think I can."

"He has no hard feelings for you anymore."

"Neither do I much for him, I think, but I still can't go along with it."

"Good enough, but the word from here is to still keep your trap shut."

"And if I don't?"

"You acting stupid again?"

"Don't you even have the slightest regret about what you do?"

"Right now no, goddamnit, no. Now what do you have to say to me but your acting stupid again?"

"I understand. I'll keep my mouth shut. And as for all the problems you caused me and your own ethics: fuck you," and I hang up.

Larry calls me a minute later and yells into the phone "Don't you ever speak to Penny like that again, don't ever, I'm warning you, don't."

"All right, take it easy, I won't," and he hangs up.

JACKIE

The badly decomposed body of an unidentified man was found floating in Billowy Bay off Motorboro Airport at 4:15 P.M. by a Port Authority police officer.

So?

Know who it is?

No.

Jackie.

Jackie?

Jackie, Jackie. Jackie Schmidt.

I see. Jackie Schmidt. Floating in Billowy Bay. What's that, a little article?

Under Area News.

And you can tell who it is just by reading this little thing in the paper?

I'd known he was thrown in there. First shot, then thrown.

Does it say anything about the man being shot?

Doesn't have to. I know.

But if he was shot, wouldn't they also say it?

They haven't found where yet, but they will.

And there can't be another unidentified man thrown in the same day? Of course not.

It doesn't have to be the same day. It takes time to get decomposed. In fact, it couldn't've been the same day.

How long you think it takes?

Days. Maybe two weeks. Badly decomposed, three. That's

when they threw Jackie in. Shot, took his clothes off, boom, in the water. Today's Thursday? Then three weeks today. It's him.

So what are we going to do about it?

What do you mean? Nothing. It's done. Jackie's dead. I knew about it. Now I read about it. I was only telling you, thinking maybe you knew and if you did, then who from? And if you didn't, that you'd probably be interested.

You mind my making an anonymous call to this paper so his wife could know?

Jackie not coming home for three weeks, she knows. So will everyone else in time.

How? He's unidentified and decomposed. And no clothes you say. Nothing at all?

Stripped clean. Wrist watch. Socks. Even his gold star.

I don't know why they didn't say nude in the newspaper, but all right. Did he also have no fingerprints on when you people threw him in?

I didn't throw anybody in. Neither do I know who did. I just know some people who know who did and why and how it went. Gambling debts. But in bad, and loans. Things like that. Worse. Taking on additional big debts with another group and not paying off the first one a dime before he did and then telling both groups to go eat it. Now if he'd just been in deep with the first people and told them to eat it, they would've only broken his arm. But taking on two big debts way way over his head and telling them both to eat it and then going to another city to take on a third, well that was too much. The first two met and, with the third's approval, decided to dump him. As for your fingerprints, I guess not. Why bother, for they'd also have to kick out all his teeth and fill in his chin cleft and scars. Besides, they didn't want to make it impossible for him to be identified.

Then you'll have to explain to me. Why only take off his clothes and in other words only go halfway with his unidentification when they know Jackie has a record and will eventually be identified? Time to give them a cover or get the people who did it away?

No. They thought it'd be a good lesson to whoever might think he can beat out on two big debts to two vaguely related groups and to tell them both to go eat it besides.

But how these people who are supposed to get the lesson supposed to find out it's a lesson and then one meant for them? By reading of an unidentified decomposed man found floating in the bay who could've gotten there through some long sleep-walk? How did the groups even know it was going to make the paper, nothing as the article was. And if they did, that it'd even be read?

Whisper and word got passed around starting a month ago. Jackie's betting. Jackie's welshing. Jackie's in very steep. Jackie won't cough up a note for them and told both of them to eat it raw. Jackie could get a leg broke talking and acting that way. If anyone's a pal of Jackie's, give him the word? Jackie's missing. Hey, anybody see Jackie or hear from him the last few days? Then, body found. Man. Hmm, bay you say? Tomorrow or the next day we'll read he'd been shot with a small-caliber bullet so close and clean that it almost got lost behind the back hairs of his head. Everybody will know who it is and what for. As for the newspaper, that's not the important thing. If it didn't get in, someone would phone them. What's more important is that the people this lesson's directed to get to know it slow.

These groups never seemed that clever to me to plan it so smooth.

Listen, we're no psychologists and know little about the subject, but in what these groups do and their customers, they are. They haven't studied it but just know.

So I'll forget my call and even thinking about it.

You'll see for yourself. Jackie's wife will claim the body in a few days and there'll be a funeral and we'll attend.

We were his such good friends and nobody will mind?

No one. Neither his wife, who'll be compensated for the lesson. And the people who did him in will even expect it of us and some of them will be there too. They play it decent, very orderly and good manners, something Jackie didn't do or have. That was his problem. Not much brains too. Hand in hand with his gambling, that can kill you. Being a smart ass besides, you're dead.

I'll remember that.

It can save your life.

Lookit, a life worth saving might as well be my own. I'll

remember that. You know, I don't think I like this business anymore. Money's good and not too many hours and so far steady,
but too much excitement for me and you never know who to
trust. Your friend's your friend one day, next day you're fingered
by him on maybe even a lie and with his or her thumb pressed
down on your throat goodbye.

There's a lot depending on it for everyone, that's why. You
just got to do what's expected of you till you get the right to
give orders and advice. That takes time and you got to want it.
No matter what, never think you're absolutely safe. Like with any
job, any business. Draw up your own parallels.

But even when you're right up there, company president and
the rest of it, do something wrong and you can get it in the head.

Not if you do nothing wrong. Everything's protected. Or let's
say, all your moves are almost already made. Sure, accidents
happen, flukes out of nowhere. New people move in, alliances
fall apart and develop, but then you got to know who to be for.
All in all though, you got to just stay in line.

But what you're saying makes it seem even more impossible.
This one, that one, time comes along how do I know I'll be dumb
enough to pick the wrong one. You saw with that phone call.
Suppose I'd dialed it and some power person found out and they
didn't like it and for all I know it could've been my third to fourth
very wrong move in a short time and they might decide I also
definitely belong away. You could've told them of all those times
I don't know about and now know in fact.

Me? Your best friend?

No trust. I can feel it. I really think I want out, but total.

Too early. You got too much put in and they with you the
same for you to go so immediately. You have to withdraw and
keep on stepping not so much in as you're withdrawing till everything you do's being done by someone else or among a crew
and you're so unnoticed you're out. Something like that. But
takes time.

Then I'm leaving the area.

Forget it. They see a small hole, means someone's missing.
You're not around, means it's you. They find out and you'll have
to explain. Once out they'll be afraid you know too much, or in
again, that you'll want out too much again no matter what your

denials and future promises to them. So they might start watching you and soon think maybe they're spending too much energy
watching you and they might take other ways. You should've
thought of all this before you came in.

How could I have known?

Come on. You heard of it, read about it, grown up with it,
since a kid seen it in the movies and still do. Well it's not so
far from all those combined where you should've known what
it was like beforehand.

Poor Jackie.

Stupid Jackie you mean.

Poor. Because he's dead. Little I knew, I liked him. Oh, let's
go to bed.

I want to read some more.

You feeling like a little physical activity tonight?

Not tonight, love, not tonight.

The article about Jackie?

It's not that.

Then good reading.

And you, sweet dreams.

THE BATTERER

My wife beats me up. Occasionally. I'm a relatively small man so she can beat me up without being afraid I'm going to beat her up back. Oh, I hit her back. Hard as I can sometimes. I got to protect myself. I'm a peaceful man and peace-loving, all that, but sometimes she gets so mad, and often over what seems the smallest thing, that she's got to take it out on something, and after she takes it out on something—a glass against the floor, tearing a piece of cloth apart—she takes it out on me. That's when I got to defend myself. I try all ways. First verbally. That sometimes works, but not usually. Then when she starts challenging me more, I walk away but she usually follows me wherever I go. When she starts swinging I try holding up my arms and deflecting her blows, but can't deflect all of them and even the ones I do deflect hurt my hands and arms.

That's when I got to stop being so peaceful and start defending myself. I hit back. I try for the blow that will incapacitate her without harming her, like in the arm where it'll hurt so much she can't swing it, but that one rarely works as my aim is never that good. When she really gets violent and uncontrollable I have to hit back hard and even aim for her belly or head. But she's much bigger than me and the harder I hit back the harder she hits me and because she hits harder than me and I'm smaller and can never get as ferocious as her, her hitting hurts me much more than mine does her.

I've gone to court about her beating me up. First time they

wouldn't even hear me. Second time I made sure to come with X-rays and my doctor's report and the judge said "You're pressing assault charges against your wife? Where is the woman?"

My wife stood up.

"Do you beat this man as he says?" Several people in the courtroom laughed and he banged his gavel for them to shut up.

"No," she said.

"That's a filthy lie," I said.

"Steady there, sir," the judge said, "or I'll get you for contempt."

"All I'm saying, Your Honor, is that she overpowers me and at times has nearly knocked me out. I never start the fights. I do everything I can to avoid and then stop them. This wound here—the one above my eye? She gave me that one two days ago."

"What about the one over my eye?" my wife shouted.

"That was in self-defense."

"Hell it was. You started it. You hit me. You tried to kill me so I swung back."

"If you don't like the treatment you get from your husband," the judge said, "why don't you move out?"

"Because I love him and all the other times he treats me very well."

"And if you don't like the treatment you say you get from her, why don't you move out?"

"I have," I said. "But for one reason or another I always go back. Probably this time I can't, or as long as she's still there or at least till something can be done about her. Because why should I move out for good and give away everything we own to her? And I like my apartment. It's cheap and cozy and where I live. If anyone's to move out, it should be her. She's the one beating me up, not the reverse."

"What are you asking of this court?"

"This is the Family Court, right? So if it wants us to stay a family then I want you to issue what I heard's called an order of protection prohibiting her from hitting me. That way I can move back with her. But if I come in here again from a beating then I want another order of protection issued forcing her to leave our apartment and never to try and see me again. If she still does after that and strikes me, then I want the court to next time get me victim's compensation for her or stick her in jail, since maybe those are the only things that will stop her from attacking me if the orders of protection don't."

"I'm sorry but your petition's denied. For one reason, you've no witness to the alleged beating and it seems that she could have just as easily pressed assault charges or asked for an order of protection against you. Secondly, this court doesn't like to interfere in domestic disputes except of the most serious kind and then mostly when it's the child or wife who gets battered by a parent or spouse. Even if your assault charge is true, I wouldn't think you'd come to this court to resolve the problem but would deal with it as a man in the privacy of your home, or just move out if you're unable to remedy things."

I tried to explain. "She's bigger than me," etcetera. "I'll end up getting killed by her if I hit her any harder than I already do to protect myself," but the judge started to laugh a little along with most of the courtroom.

I always take a hotel room after a bad beating and have always moved back. She sends me flowers and love letters and poems. I've heard of men batterers doing some of those things to get their wives back and there have been TV programs on it also—fictional and documentary and in the news—so maybe that's where she got the idea of those love gifts and romantic apologetic phone calls, though I'm almost sure she was sincere about them each of those last times.

But after a few weeks of this she always convinces me she'll never hit me again and, if anything, just a little love tap but nothing much harder than that. And when I go back, out of loneliness also, we usually have a normal life together for a few months. Kindness and sympathy and affection and even deep feelings and passion for one another, before something would happen. She'd ask me, as she did the last time, if I saw the thing she was searching for in the apartment, and if I said something just a little bit contentious like "Why should I?" or "You're always losing things around the house," as I might be very tired or just not feeling too good that day myself, she'd come right back with something like "Listen, I don't want to get into an argument about it. All I asked was if you saw it and if you didn't, don't give me any of that cynical crap back."

"I'm sorry."

"You're always sorry. Just don't do it again."

"I'm not always sorry and it's possible I might do it again. I'm just sorry this time for having said it and maybe making you even angrier. Because I can see you're in a foul mood."

"I'll really be in a foul mood if you keep that cynical chattering up."

"I'm not cynically chattering. Maybe the first thing I said was snappy, which I apologize for, but I'm now speaking reasonably to you. Anyway, when you're in a bad mood like this almost nothing will get you out of it, so mind if we drop the subject?"

"Yes I mind—a lot. I want to get this thing out into the open once and for all."

"Get what? You're just baiting me, can't you see? I haven't got enough scars on my face to let you know why I don't want to start up with you again?"

"You have to bring that up? My hitting you when you always started those fights, that's what argument you're going to use?"

"Forget it, this is ridiculous," and I go into the bedroom. She follows me.

"You're not going to stop I see," I say.

"No I'm not. I want to know why you had to bring up the fights when that wasn't what I had in mind."

"I know it's not in your mind. But it's what always happens when you get excited like this. You get into some wild emotional or mental state or both that winds up with you physically lashing out at me uncontrollably."

"Oh and you're in such perfect control. You're so perfectly normal. So damn sensitive and controlled."

"Those used to be qualities you liked in me. Just a few weeks ago you said it too."

"I was lying."

"Then don't say it next time."

"Don't tell me what to say or not say. But saying anything to you is a mistake. You're my life's curse, you know that? I never should've hooked up with you."

"Then unhook me, okay? I won't protest. But what I'll never be able to understand is why you get into moods like this that are almost over nothing and then insist on harping on the same theme or any theme just to get me to verbally fight with you when it's obvious I don't want to. Now stop, will you?"

"I'll verbally you. I'll stop you. I'll smack your damn ugly head off with my fist, that's how I'll verbally stop you."

"Now none of that. I don't want to go to court again. The judge'll believe me next time."

"He'll call you a faggot next time. A prissy little whimpery faggot and then laugh even harder in your face, that's what he'll do."

"The hell with reasoning with you then," and I get down on my knees to pull a valise out from under the bed.

"What're you doing?"

"Getting away, that you can bet. I'm not hanging around here waiting for you to drive a wedge into my head."

"Why, you too much the whimpery coward to stand up and talk back to me like a man?"

"Yes."

"You are, I was right, you faggot, so why didn't you say what your hang-ups were when you first met me and saved me the trouble of hooking up with you?"

"The truth is that talking to you doesn't work when you get like this and that's the last time I'm going to tell you that, the last."

"You saying something's wrong with my personality?"

"What are you, kidding me? Yes, goddamnit, I am."

"You bastard, you coward, you make me so mad I could bash your face in, I really could, you bastard, coward, faggot," and she swings at me and I duck and jump to my feet to protect myself but she connects with the next. Right to the mouth. I fly across the bed and a couple of my teeth I think fly someplace else. She weighs maybe fifty pounds more than me and has three inches on me too. She drags me off the bed by my feet and I land on my rear and she kicks me in the ribs. That really hurts and I'm spitting blood besides but I get up and she swings and I block her blow and hit her in the chest and that's all I had to do because now she's all over me with punches, screaming, swinging wildly, connecting every third or fourth time and before I know it she lands one to my jaw that knocks me to the floor. I feel sick. She's on top of me punching my face and hitting every time. All good shots. Nothing wild now. I can't protect myself. My whole face feels paralyzed and I want to throw up. I begin retching. She gets off me and says "That ought to teach you, you whimpering so-forth, you baby," and leaves the room and I hear the front door slam.

I'm really out of it this time. She never did a better job on me. I have to turn over and spit out a mouthful of blood to stop from gagging. I rest a while and then crawl to the bathroom to see how bad it is and get a towel to stop the bleeding on my face. My face is a mess. Some of the welts have gashes on them, probably from her rings. I stop the bleeding in my mouth by sticking a rolled-up ball of wet toilet paper between my front teeth and upper lip. I wash myself, smear several streaks of iodine across my face and on my ears and when I feel steady enough I call my best friend.

"Herb, could you come over? Melanie really did a number on me this time. I might have to go to the hospital I think."

"I'll phone for an ambulance and run right over. Rest till I get there. Door unlocked?"

"I think so. Wow, my mouth hurts. I don't see her suddenly being so considerate to think of locking the door so burglars can't come in. If not, landlord's got the keys. I doubt I can get to the door myself."

I rest in bed. Herb comes with his wife in minutes. They wash my face and head and Debra says "Anything broken you think?"

"Maybe something in my chest. She kicked me. I think I blanked out but do remember a certain thumping going on down there when I was on the floor, but can't tell for sure. It now feels numb."

"We told you not to go back to her."

"I wasn't thinking. Believe me, never again."

"You do, you lose us as friends."

"I know. Thanks."

"If only she'd done it once when we were with you," Herb says, "you'd have had that witch in a sling by now and could have skipped all this."

"No chance. She's too careful that way. But maybe I got her this time only because of the extent of the beating and condition of my face."

Ambulance comes and takes me away. I'm examined. I have two broken ribs and a broken nose and cheekbone and concussion and have lost all my hearing in one ear and several missing teeth. I'm kept in the hospital for weeks. I ask to see the police and learn they also want to see me. She's pressed charges that I got drunk that night and tried to kill her. I tell them that's bull and press countercharges against her. My lawyer tells me "The best you can get from this is that if you drop charges against her, she'll drop hers against you. She's got too strong a case." And he reads me what she told the police: "He's an erratic drunk. Not a regular drinker as our friends will tell you, but once every other month at home he drinks too much and falls all over the place banging his head and face, which is how he cut his ears and such and lost the teeth. I even picked up the teeth this time to show him what he was doing to himself, but threw them out the window when he rushed at me like a mad dog. For when he gets drunk like that he also occasionally goes berserk and throws things and slaps out at anything in his way. Since I live with him, who else you think gets the brunt? And let's not be silly— you think I'd hit that man first? He might be a little smaller than me but he's wiry and quick and powerful and once or twice in the past he hit me so good that I wouldn't ever think of tangling with him except if I couldn't get out of the house and it was fight him or lose my life. That's what happened this time. The other times he battered me, though I never told our friends or even the ones who are just his friends and maybe believe him, because I was too ashamed and let's face it, the man supports me, and never reported him to you because I knew he'd really give me a licking after that. And then every time after that he moves away out of remorse and in a few weeks pleads with me to take him back. I always did as I'm a sucker for such slob talk and do depend on him for a lot of things and I'm not so young and pretty where I can get another guy that quick and also when he isn't so violently drunk like that he can be very sweet, but from now on I won't."

My lawyer says "The court will believe her rather than you

which they always do in cases like this when the evidence isn't entirely in your favor. Besides, even if they've doubts you weren't lying, to most people the man's supposed to fight back. Please, whatever you do from now on, stay clear of her."

I drop charges, she drops hers, I'm ordered by the court to send her a certain sum of money every week if I'm going to live apart, and I move into a hotel, start looking for an apartment and, because of the notoriety our situation got, my boss asks me to look for another job. Month later Melanie calls and says "Thanks for this week's check."

"You're welcome."

"It's nice speaking to you again."

"It isn't for me."

"I want us to get back together, what do you say?"

"That last time was the last time of all the times and I never want to see or speak to you again," and hang up.

She calls back. "I promise the past won't be repeated. I got it all out of my system. I love you, need you, want you—please. Don't you even still like me a little bit and think of me or my body some? Don't you ever want to hold me again or want me to wrap myself around you at night like I used to and cuddle you to sleep?"

"Sometimes I think of you. I'll be honest. And not just think of you negatively. There were good times, yes, but when you got the adrenaline going till you turned into some horrible beast— well what do you think I am, permanently insane? Next time you'll kill or maim me to where I'll never again be able to stand. No. Definitely not."

"What can I do to make you change your mind and see how much I changed?"

"Nothing."

"Please. I can hear it in your voice. What? Tell me. For you I'll do anything."

"Two things for sure, though even then I can't promise I'll come back. One, tell the district attorney's office you did assault me those last few times and that I didn't strike you first. That way they won't think I'm making up stories and my boss and clients won't think I'm a little crazy. Then, if you beat me again, the city can also send you away or fine you or whatever they do to repeated offenders."

"No. They'll get me for perjury for swearing out untrue charges against you and maybe throw me in jail."

"Two, you have to start therapy right away. Group and individual both. And also go to a religious adviser every week to declare that you beat me repeatedly and nearly killed me last time and to keep going till they tell me you worked it out."

"I can't. People will think the worst things of me. It's crazy for a woman to be called a husband batterer. Society won't tolerate it. They'll say I'm wicked or insane and give me drugs or put me away. They'll also think I married a queer. A whimpering milquetoast. I don't want them to think that. I don't want them to think I married a man who can't stand up to anyone."

"You have my two stipulations."

"I can't meet them."

"Then that's it then, goodbye."

"But I swear I won't hit you again. Sweetheart, please, I love you, come home right now. I'll make it nice. I'll bathe you, make your favorite foods, take care of you in every way, do everything you want me to, take gladly all your commands."

"I don't want to command. I just wanted our relationship to be natural as possible, no fakeries or postures, can't you see? Beating isn't natural. Getting things out of your system is, but not like you do. Yours is vicious. Sadistic. You don't even stop when I'm down. No, first work out your problems or at least show me you've begun to by telling the district attorney's office and going to that therapy thing for a month. Only then I'll come back."

"If you don't come back now I'm really going to get mad."

"What, break my neck?"

"Yes."

"There, see? Oh, I wish I had a recording of this call. Forget it," and I hang up.

Hour later she knocks on my hotel-room door. I say through the peephole "Go away or I'll call the desk."

"What'll you say: 'My wife wants to get into my room'?"

"Yes, I'll say that. Also that you want to murder me, that you tried it before and nearly succeeded and that I want protection from you."

"You don't need protection. I only want to speak gently to you."

"No."

She kicks the door. I say "Save your energy, I'm not opening up." She bangs her shoulder against the door. I say "I'm calling them so you better leave."

She's still banging. A paint seam runs down the entire middle of the door and the wood seems to be buckling. I call downstairs.

"Manager? Then assistant then, listen. There's a woman at my door who's my wife, all right, but we're legally separated and she's trying to get in my room to kill me, I'm not kidding. She won't go away. She's busting down the door now. Get up here. 6G. She's a very big woman and I just recently got out of the hospital from a serious beating from her and I'm not allowed to get excited and certainly not to fight back."

They come upstairs. She yells "Let me go. He has someone in there—a prostitute, that's why I'm here."

"That true, Mr. Ridge?" a man says through the door.

"Absolutely not."

"I myself saw him accost her on the street before and ride the elevator up with her. I'm reporting this hotel for allowing whores in it."

"She's lying. I've no one. She's just trying to get in the room to attack me. Call the police, Fifth Precinct, Sergeant Abneg if he's in or any of his associates and ask them if they don't have a file on us about this beating thing."

"Could you open the door so we can see for ourselves? If you do have a woman in there, for one thing it's a single room and she's not a paying guest, and for another, if she is a prostitute then we'll have to ask you and the woman in there to leave. We don't allow that in this hotel."

"I told you. My wife just wants to get in here."

"Then we'll have to open the door ourselves. Sergio, the passkey."

They get the key in a minute and open the door. I'm at the other end of the room with a chair raised over my head ready to bring it down on her if she makes a move toward me. She screams "You whoremonger," and rushes at me. I bring the chair down. It hits her shoulder and she falls and gets up, drops again and while the two men are keeping me from hitting her again with the chair, she gets up and grabs an ashtray off a table and smashes it against my head. I go down.

"Ma'am," one of the men says.

She kicks me in the jaw. I hear the snap and know it's broken. She kicks it again and again and I go out. Next thing I know I'm in an ambulance driving through the city, a doctor leaning over me holding open one of my eyes.

I press charges against my wife from the hospital bed. The policewoman I speak to says "Your wife claims you had a prostitute in your room."

I can't speak but write on a pad: "She lies. I didn't."

"You might've that evening, as your wife said she distinctly saw you solicit a woman on the street and take her into your hotel and that's what got her so mad to knock on your room door."

I write: "Lies, lies, lies."

"The court will tend to believe her. If not for the prostitute, who you could've gotten rid of before your wife got upstairs, then that she broke your jaw in self-defense. She's witnesses to that."

I write: "Hit her with chair for frightened death of her that's why. She phoned hour before, said she'd kill me when she got to hotel."

"You'll never be believed. It's not my job to suggest this, but drop the charges."

I don't. Case is thrown out of court. I later file for divorce, charging physical cruelty. My wife fights the divorce and wins. At the courtroom she's so soft-spoken and sweet. Tells the judge I drink and beat her up every few months, etcetera. "But I still love him, don't ask me why after all he's put me through, and want him back."

I get a legal separation and file for divorce the long way and even then it might not be granted if she doesn't stop challenging it. "If you do get it despite her fighting it," my lawyer says, "you'll have to give her everything you own and more alimony a year than you now earn and which you'll have to continue giving even if she remarries."

I get my own apartment and go back to work. Melanie calls three to four times a week. She pleads with me to come back.

I always hang up. Sometimes she follows me on the street, waits outside my office building and apartment house for me. I always get in a cab or duck into a subway and escape. She writes me ardent letters saying how she misses me, cries every night for me, wants me to make love to her, wants me to give her a child, letters like that. I rip them all up and eventually don't even open them.

I try and think of a way to get her to take one last unprovoked swing at me in front of witnesses. Then I could charge her with assault and maybe win this time and also get a quick divorce because of her physical cruelty and a legal writ preventing her from seeing and speaking to me again. But why bother, because the judge would probably say her hitting me again was caused by all the past times I'd provoked her. I'm also afraid that the next time she hits me she might batter my brains or eyes so much that I'd become blind or knocked into insensibility for good.

About six months after our courtroom battle and a few weeks after she stopped calling and sending letters, I get a phone call.

"It's me, don't hang up," she says. "I want to give you a quick uncontested divorce."

"What's the trick now?"

"No trick, darling, it's love. I met a beautiful man and we want to get married."

"I hope he's a foot taller and a hundred pounds heavier than you."

"He happens to be even thinner and shorter than you, but don't be mean."

"I can see why you want to marry him. So you can beat him up even worse than you did me."

"Not true."

"Don't tell me."

"And don't argue with me either. You want the divorce or not? Don't grant me it and you'll never see the end of me for a lifetime."

"I want it."

We agree to file for divorce on the grounds of mutual mental cruelty. We get the divorce in a month, and a week later she marries. I saw the man at the divorce court. He's a little guy all right, older and weaker-looking than me too. I wanted to warn him about her but then told myself to stay out of it. It's his business. And if I say anything he might not marry her and then she'll be on my back for life. Besides, if she does beat him up and he presses charges, the court and most of my old friends will know I wasn't crazy after all. Two men pressing assault charges against the same woman—that's no coincidence.

A year later she and her husband are in the newspaper. He's in a very bad coma. His sister, the article says, got a call from her brother saying Melanie was trying to break down their bedroom door to attack him. When the sister got to the apartment she found her brother on the floor and Melanie kicking him repeatedly in the head. The sister tore into her, knocked her out with a pan and then called the hospital and police.

Melanie's arrested. Her husband's still in a coma. A newsman calls me and says "Mrs. Delray's your ex-wife. So what do you think of the charges against her now—husband battering, attempted murder? Where it might end up a homicide, as he's got no more than a fifty-fifty chance to survive. Even if he does she'll still be in serious trouble, as he hasn't got any chance of being anything but totally brain-damaged for the rest of his life."

"If you don't mind I'll save what I have to say for the jury trial. Because I might be prejudicing the case if I told you all that happened to me and then because of some legal technicality she got away free," and I hang up.

A LACK OF SPACE

They never let me out in the sun anymore. I don't know why. My lawyer and I have never gotten a clear ruling on that. But when night comes and it's dark, I'm allowed a ten-minute rest period outside. There I see the other suns—the stars. I learned that from some library books here and the newspaper articles I've been reading regarding this country's space effort. The other stars are supposed to be suns, like ours, though in varying degrees of intensity depending on how big they are and how long they've been around. And every one of the other suns is capable of having its own solar system and our sun is only one of about one hundred billion in our galaxy and there are about five thousand galaxies in our cluster of galaxies and we're all revolving together because we're all held together by the force of gravitational pull each galaxy in our cluster exerts on the other, despite the fact that the closest galaxy to ours is two million light-years away from us and each light-year is approximately six trillion miles in length, and actually all of us—Earth, solar system, galaxy and cluster of galaxies—may be part of an even larger system called a cluster of clusters of galaxies, though because of limitations in astronomical equipment scientists haven't discovered it yet. Meaning: no matter how big we think the universe is, it's probably even bigger than that. Meaning: no matter how many billions of trillions of light-years of space we know about or can imagine going in every which direction starting from Earth, there's probably trillions of trillions of times more space than that. So why do these prison officials have to be so petty as to deny me a relatively small sun to look at and which they know is what I like to look at and do almost most, and particularly in its setting state? And why only the night for ten minutes to see those other suns? Because I'm a condemned man, they probably reason, and they got to deny me more than the usual prison freedoms they deny the other men on death row, since I once committed that most heinous crime of all of making hay with a girl who was a minor and when she was through with me and tying her hair in back with a ribbon she said "God, if you're not the worst lay in all these creations, then I don't know who is," and kept on repeating that opinion in various ways till I said lay off and she wouldn't so I insulted her a bit and she said "Goddamn you, fag, you can't go insulting me like that," and still nude she grabbed a branch and came at me as if she was going to cream me with it, so I slapped it out of her hand and shoved her with my palm just to protect myself from the rock she was picking up and she fell back over her own foot and banged her head against the top of a tree stump and rolled off it onto some stones just as I leaped forward to stop her from rolling and falling, and knocked herself out and died. I knew I was in trouble and there was nothing I could do for her now, so I beat it out of there and someone found her soon after and the police came and the doctors at the hospital said she had been viciously attacked and carnally assaulted and some people in town said she was last seen riding off with me on the back of my motorcycle and I was picked up and charged with rape, murder and running away from the scene of a crime. I was jailed and written up in newspapers as a young mad killer and charged with the rape-murders of three other girls in the area, though those charges didn't stand up, and brought to trial for the rape-murder of one Jenny Lou House and convicted and sentenced to die by hanging. For three years now I've had a stay of execution, since the state I was tried in has a law saying the crime I was convicted of carries a mandatory death penalty, and my lawyer who's against capital punishment on any grounds except treason and for someone who kills a federal employee who's on duty, even a postman, contends that that state law is unconstitutional. It's taken him the three years to get my case to the

nation's highest court and in all that time I've never once seen
the sun. And when I am allowed out in the high-walled six-by-
six-foot space for my ten-minute rest period, I'm always accom-
panied by two guards with guns—as if I could ever escape to
any other place but my adjoining locked cell—and the space is
always brightly lit as a main city square might be, making it
impossible some nights to see the stars.

I wish I had another chance. If I did I would never shove
another girl, or at least not till I first married her. I think a
married man has less chance of being sentenced to death for
killing his wife rather than a girl he recently met, even if he
confesses to the charge, which I didn't since the girl I supposedly
raped and murdered was actually the one who seduced and
nearly murdered me. I met her in this doughnut place she was
countergirling at and it wasn't a minute after I settled on the
stool that she said "That your bike?" meaning my motorcycle in
the lot, and I said yes and she said "When do you get off work?"
and I told her I'm not working now, only riding, and she said
"That was intended as a play on words, young man, as what I
meant is when do you want to take me for a ride around this
dinky town and maybe even out of it?" and I said I really don't
like putting girls on my back who aren't at least twenty-one and
who also know how to sway with the rider, meaning leaning right
when I go right and so on, and she said "I'm twenty-one except
I look older from working in this nut house and living in another,
and I've been on the backs of more riders than we have dough-
nuts in this shop, and besides I once owned a bike myself and
if I still had it I could outride you from here to the Coast by
a day and a half." "Bull," I said. "Buy me a bike and I'll prove
it," she said. "Ha," I said. "Want a free cof and French jelly?" she
said. "You're something," I said. "And you're something for saying
I'm something, and also for having such a big beautiful bike. Now
what time did you say you got off work?" "Seven?" I said. "That's
about the time I lay off also," and she told me to meet her at
the corner across the street, not here in front. "This is a small
town with big mouths and I don't want my folks knowing I'm
going with riders again. And here—no one's looking," and she
slipped me a bag filled with French jellies and two containers
of chocolate fizz.

That night I met her at the corner. She ran her hand over the chromium fenders and carb pipes and said "Wow, this is really one striking gorgeous creature you're keeping," and was all set to straddle the back when a man walked past. She turned on me winking and said "Excuse me, mister, but I don't talk to strange customers no matter how big a tip they leave or promise next time—oh, hello, Mr. Denham." "Hello, Jenny Lou," the man said, "anything wrong?" "Nothing I can't handle thanks very much, and give my best regards to Mrs. Denham and Beverly." "I'll convey them that," he said, still eyeing me suspiciously as he walked away. He was a friend of her folks, according to the newspapers, and one of the last persons to see Miss House alive. He later identified me in court as "That's right, the one with the snarl," when at that moment of identification I was despondent near to tears, and gave evidence how he heard me annoying Jenny Lou on the street and tried to warn her about me but she said she knew perfectly well how to handle the situation. "Well apparently she didn't," Mr. Denham said, "or else this young man was crafty enough to handle the situation a lot more perfectly than she." The judge told the clerk to strike Mr. Denham's last remark from the record and for the jury to disregard it when they make a final decision. But I could see from their faces they wouldn't. They all had me hung from the start.

"Are you going to exchange how-do-you-dos with distrusting townsmen," I said, "or are you coming riding with me?" "I'm going to do better than that," Jenny said. "I'm going to ride out with you some quiet place and hump you there till you're black and blue all over and then I'm going to leave you for dead when all you'll be is dead tired from my humping and steal your bike and ride it to the Coast and put it on a boat for the Orient and ride it across that continent and maybe even via China if she'll have me and then across the Mideast and Africa and Europe and back on a boat and then ride it halfway across the country to home again. I expect that whole trip to take me a couple of years, wouldn't you think?" "You scare me," I said. "You got these wild nutty ideas which I even think you want to carry out some. I don't believe you're not jailbait anymore. Let me see your driver's license." "I don't have one," she said, "because I once got busted and put away for riding a bike into a crowd when I was seventeen

and the police took away both my license and bike. Two people
got killed, that's why." "Then some form of identification," I said,
but all she'd brought with her was a five-dollar bill, just in case
I left her stranded and she had to get a ride home. "What year
were you born—quickly now: what year?" and she gave the date
for someone born twenty-one years ago. I knew too well about
getting girls any younger on my back. Besides the possible trouble with police over curfews and such, these girls had tendencies
to scream bloody murder if they suddenly got cross with you and
sometimes for no better reason than your not wanting to go a
hundred-fifty miles an hour in a thirty-mile-an-hour zone. The
younger they are beginning with the day after their sweet-sixteen
party, the faster they want to ride. And I later learned from my
lawyer that Jenny had only two months before I met her turned
sixteen. She probably mastered my age test because she had
failed the same test with some other rider who had put it to
her. If I ever get out of here I would think of a totally new test
which for all I knew only I had the answer to. And after I used
it on the first girl I didn't think was twenty-one, I'd think up
another new test for the next girl I didn't think was twenty-one—
always a new test so it could never get circulated and known.

"Hop on, Miss Twenty-one," I said, and she got on behind
me, squeezed into me tighter than she had to to hold on. Nipped
my ear with her teeth after we took a sharp corner and hugged
my chest as we rode till I could hardly take in air. "I saw him
force her on his motorcycle," her boss, Mr. Hill, said at my trial.
"He was having rape and murder on his mind even then," Mrs.
Hill told the jury. "Strike that out, clerk," the judge said. "Jury
will disregard witness's last remark. Witness will be encouraged
not to offer opinions of what went on in the defendant's mind,
but to restrict her answers only to what she observed the last
time she saw defendant and the deceased." "But that is what
I observed," Mrs. Hill said. "I remember telling my husband Mr.
Hill as I looked at those two from my shop—'Paul,' I said, 'that
young man has rape and murder on his mind if I ever saw one.'"
My lawyer objected. The jury was instructed and the witness
reproached. "I'm sorry," Mrs. Hill said, "I wasn't thinking just now.
But I suppose you can't help me for having bad feelings toward
that man, since Jenny Lou was such a nice pretty girl and the

most dependable worker we ever had. Murderer," she yelled, and the judge banged his gravel till I thought it would split. "Rapist. Riffraff. Beggar. Scum."

I asked Jenny if she could take me to the most beautiful spot in the area and she said "There's a nice site by the river only twelve miles from here, but that's too close." "That's distance enough for me," I said. "I've ridden four hundred miles today and I'm nearly done in." "Well I want to ride more than that," she said, "and there's another site sixty miles up along the same river that's just as pretty. Let's drive there," and "Please?" and "Oh come on, just this once," so I gave in and we got on the bike again and it was during this ride I really began thinking she was under twenty-one because all she wanted to do was go faster, faster. When I was doing sixty she wanted eighty and when I was doing eighty she said get it up to a hundred and when I reached a hundred she said one-ten, that's all, just one-ten and she won't ask for no more, but I pretended not to hear and even slowed down to ninety. I was getting worried she would fall off in all her excitement with the ride, and also of the police. You never knew for sure when they'd be hiding behind a board.

"I only got a chance to see them because they had to slow down for an ell-turn," Conrad Jenkins, insurance broker, told the court, "and let me tell you I've never seen a girl looked so frightened in her life. It seemed she wanted desperately to get off the motorcycle while he at the same time I was seeing them from my picnic table was doing everything that sort knew to keep her on." The judge cautioned Mr. Jenkins and Mr. Jenkins apologized and said he should have known better. "Having been an adjustor for hundreds of accident cases I know that witnesses are up here not to give their opinions or condemnations, but to confine their answers to the objective facts alone. But that was how I felt. I never saw a girl look so frightened, and in my work experience I've seen a lot."

"What do you think of my site?" Jenny said when we reached the river, and I told her it's beautiful and it was. No houses to be seen, no bridges, factories or boats. Just a quiet broad river with trees bordering both sides of it and beyond the trees were hills, mountains, clouds and a setting sun lighting up the edges of the clouds like what? Like a painting. Up till then I hadn't been sure a place like that existed. It was what I started out traveling for, what I had even learned how to ride a bike for. To get off to the more primitive remote places people hardly go to anymore because they either don't want to or these places are too tough to get to except by bike or Land-rover. I took off my boots and walked in a ways and asked Jenny if she'd mind my going in for a dip in only my underpants as I didn't want to wet my blue jeans, and she said "Take everything off if you want to, I as sure don't care. In fact, I'm going to take everything off also and then scrub us down with soap if you have any in your bag." I said I don't need a washing: the water in the river will make me clean enough. "As a matter of fact the water's going to make me pure, that's what it's going to do, because this is the purest river I've ever seen. Oh, I love your place, Jenny Lou," and I stripped to my underpants and jumped in the river and coming up from around a minute's swimming underwater I got what was the most beautiful view I ever saw: the setting sun reflecting off the water all around me, making it look like a river of pure golden honey I was in. Jenny came up from the water right beside me, nothing on her, looking great too. I said "Know how man first thought there was something like a Supreme Being around him?" and she said "Oh, you're one of those." "One of what?" I said, very cheerful, "it's just something I discovered now myself for whatever it's worth—want to hear?" She said, both of us treading water, "Okay—how?" and I said "Very long ago a man drove sixty miles by cart or went six miles by foot but did something to get here but got here and dove underwater and came up after a minute at this exact same time of the day on this exact same day and month of that year to the exact same weather and site we're seeing right now and said '*God*.'" She said "That's nice, I like that," and kissed me on the nose, which I liked her doing. "Now let's swim around some and then get out before we get chilled," and I said "Good idea, Jenny, my friend," and dived down and pulled on her legs till she was underwater with me and kissed her on the forehead. Then we swam around till the sun set and then swam back to land.

"Her body was bruised and scratched and appeared, by my best medical expertise, to have been beaten both before and after she was raped," the coroner told the judge. "Please speak to the jury, Doctor," the judge said. "Well as I said just now, she had bruises and lacerations around her pelvic region, thighs, abdomen, buttocks, breasts and neck, her head suffered several severe concussive blows with a blunt instrument such as a jack iron or baseball bat and she seemed, according to my post-mortem examination, to have been savagely beaten both before and after she was sexually attacked—beaten till she was either dead or left for dead but if left for dead then in a condition bordering very close to what we define as clinically dead." I never told the jurors that Jenny and I didn't make love. I never said I didn't have any idea she was a minor. I even told them about that ridiculous age test I gave her and how more and more during the ride to the river I thought she was sixteen instead of twenty-one. I told them everything. I told them I only shoved her in self-defense and she lost her footing and that the whole bad scene of name-calling and branch-wielding and then the accident and death had actually started because Jenny didn't think I was a good lover. But I still didn't shove her for that, I swore. I only did it because she was going to come at me with a rock.

"You don't seem to want to do anything," Jenny said, both of us snuggled up comfy and warm at the water's edge under my bedroll. "You're not even excited." "You checked?" I said. "I don't have to check but will if you're too numb to know it natural yourself." She pulled the bedroll off us and looked. "Nothing. Is it because you're impotent or hate girls?" "Maybe I don't feel like it tonight. Let me for now lie quiet and look at the stars and feel good with everything about life and just hold you for a while. I like it here, Jenny. It's a very nice place you brought me to and I'll always be thankful for that. I've never seen the sun go down like that ever. Did you see the way it lit up and colored the sky and made the clouds almost seem like cotton balls on fire? It was like a religious scene in a movie where the whole heavens open up and the organ music begins. Or something like such. Words can't come close to the experiencing of it and I never knew that better than now." "Don't you like me?" she said. "Sure I like you, but that doesn't have to be important to you now, does it?" "You're damn right it does. And if I'm going to lay with a guy then I want him to like me or I can't do it." "Then don't do it. Let's be truthful and open about it. If we do it then we do it

only because we want to and if we both want to do it then it'll
be fun and beautiful and good. And now I just don't want to
do it." She said "You know, I'm convinced now there's something
definitely peculiar about you. I think you're maybe a fruit who
gets his kicks by setting up girls for sex so he can put them down
when he gets them there, just to make them feel frustrated and
like dirty evil females. That's you all over." "Have it your own
way," I said. "That isn't my way—it's yours. You're the dirty evil
unnatural man, not me the woman. I'm natural. I'm natural because I want to make love." So mechanically we began to make
love. I did all the things I usually do when starting but Jenny
did much more than that. She really went into a frenzy, panting
and screaming and tearing away with her hands at both our
bodies and getting me kind of excited though not that excited
but still excited enough to make me want to continue beyond
the point where I was planning to say "You see, I was right
before: nothing. I just don't feel like it tonight, though you can't
say I didn't at least try." I couldn't imagine what she'd do if she
really loved some man who really loved her. Maybe nothing very
much. But she howled and kicked and rolled us all over the
ground, which no doubt accounted for the bruises and lacerations she didn't get in her tree-stump fall, and moved herself like
no girl I'd ever been with. She kept yelling "Motorcycle man, oh
my Mr. Motorcycle Man, oh I really dig dig dig dig my Mr. Motorcycle Man." She didn't taste from alcohol so for all I know
she might have been on drugs. The coroner said no when questioned about it by my lawyer, but maybe he hadn't looked and
was only covering up himself to keep his lifetime job. Or maybe
she just liked men better than any girl I'd ever known or heard
about. She was like out of a dime novel when they sold for a
quarter and I used to read them under my covers by flashlight
when I was a kid and my folks were asleep. Or like the girls on
detective and true romance magazines with the title in first person underneath about them being uncontrollable or incurable
nymphomaniacs. Because whatever I did for Jenny or she for
herself was never enough, though I didn't worry about that much.
I figured that in the morning, after we rested and I drove her
home, I'd start out West on my bike, very early. Jenny wasn't
someone to stay around for because first of all she wouldn't let

me have my thoughts and peaceful moments, and secondly she probably wouldn't want me to stay around.

"I heard her screaming—or a girl's voice screaming—at approximately nine at night at River's Point on July 26th of this year," Mr. Stevenson Smith said on the stand. "My boy was with me at the time. We were looking for our dog, Peacock, who that same afternoon jumped out of the car window when Jimmy and I were fishing. And when we heard that poor girl screaming like she was being maliciously raped—" "Objection, Your Honor." "I mean viciously raped." "Objection, Your Honor." "When we heard a girl screaming—is that all right?" "That's fine, Mr. Smith," the judge said. "Well Jimmy got so scared he ran back into the woods. I wanted to run and see what the screaming was about, but I also didn't want Jimmy disappearing like Peacock did, so I went after the boy. I found him back in the car, doors locked and windows up tight, and with the car keys in the glove compartment. I had to tell him through the side vent to calm down for I wanted to see what the trouble was with that screaming voice. Coaxing him to calm down took a while because he's a very emotional boy, very sensitive, and when he heard that screaming he, like me, didn't know what to think. He said 'No, don't go, poppa.' I said 'I have to go, Jimmy. Some lady might be in trouble, so I've got to help.' He said 'Please don't go, Poppa, I don't want to be left alone.' So I told him 'Then unlock the door, Jimmy, and come with me.'" "Get to the point, Mr. Smith." "The point is that I eventually did go back, though without Jimmy, and by this time the girl was no longer screaming. Nobody was screaming. Everything was quiet. And there she was on the grass without any clothes on and her hair combed back nice and tight and her head smashed in and blood all over the ground and her and bruised so bad I wanted to throw up. I felt if I'd have got there a half-minute sooner I could've saved that girl. I could've, you know, if my son wasn't so emotional, so sensitive. It upset him so much he's now taking pills to stay reasonably in control of himself." "Thank you, Mr. Smith. Does the State have any further witnesses?" It had none. They already paraded about fifteen against me. There wasn't anyone to say anything good about me. Just letters from my hometown that my lawyer read in court saying what a pleasant child I was when I was three and five and eight and ten but nobody had anything good to say about me after that. "A very slow worker"—an ex-boss. "Never liked to take orders"—another ex-boss. "Intelligent but with proclivities toward temper tantrums and occasional furious rages"—a grade-school teacher. "Too self-assured with no self-restraint."—a junior-high-school teacher. "Kind of creepy and slimy most times but definitely not like a murderer"—the girl I was once engaged to. "Showed tremendous potential in the beginning, but once he got involved with motorcycles I just gave up on him"—my high-school football coach. "Unstable"—my mother. "Though do have pity on him," she said from a thousand miles away, "as he's my only child and I have no one else for support." Except for the hundred thousand dollar insurance policy my dad left and which she refused to give me a cent of when I was accepted into college. "Guilty"—the jury. "Hanged till you are dead"—the judge. "They'll never hang you because the state law is unconstitutional"—my lawyer. That was three years ago. I'm still in the death cellblock and there are no windows in my cell and I'm never allowed out in the sunlight and I never get any real earth to walk on and there are ten other men here who are also waiting to see how the Supreme Court deals with my case, since each of their death sentences will be affected by the decision. None of them is very hopeful. And if the court does decide the state's execution law is constitutional, then I'll be the first to go. None of these men likes to talk about the sun and stars and galaxies with me. They say "What's the difference?" They say "So what, a star's a star." They're interested in our men walking on the moon though—very proud that fellow human beings from our own country can do that. They like to watch it each time it happens on television and also all kinds of television movies and soap operas and ball games and a few of the funnier commercials—but that's all. They actually don't like to discuss anything with me—they think it might be bad luck. So I mostly talk to myself. I say "Let me out." I plead "I didn't do anything wrong to justify being here." I shout "All I did was shove a girl. Lots of men have shoved girls and they're not in prison. She fell back over her own foot and so in a sense killed herself. She already came at me once with a branch. She was going to come at me with a rock. Now who would stand still and let his head get hit by a rock? Would you stand still? And you there, would you stand still? Oh knock it off. Because none of you would. You say so, you might think so, but all of you would have probably done worse than me. You probably would have beaten her up. And then maybe raped her after you knocked her unconscious to the ground." And I think about the sunsets I haven't seen these past three years. And that last holy sunset I saw with Jenny Lou. My traveling would probably be over by now, I think. I'd probably be married—and maybe with a baby—to a girl I loved very much and who didn't always interfere with my quietest thoughts.

"You can take your rest period," guard Vernon says, coming into my cell with guard Simms, both of them armed. They walk me to the adjoining six-by-six-foot outdoor space. I look up at the other suns—the stars. It's a clear night. The Big and Little Dippers are easily recognizable. Even the Andromeda galaxy can be seen. I've read all the prison astronomy books several times. I can identify every star formation on both sides of the equator, every significant star. I can make out planets. I can tell exactly what day of the year it is by how the stars are arranged. I could guide myself across any continent or body of water and come to the point a few thousand miles away I originally intended to get to just by following the stars. I could do all that. I learned all that here by myself. This outdoor cell is surrounded by walls several feet above my reach and on top of these walls are electric wires and there are lights all around my yard making the stars tonight a little tough to see and the two guards sit in the yard while I stand and if I stop for a second they always tell me to keep moving, now keep it moving, but the view is still something. My lawyer says the court ruling should come on my test case in a minimum of two years. He's very hopeful the state's mandatory death penalty law will be declared unconstitutional and that with a few years off for good behavior and a governor's pardon I ought to be out of here by the time I'm sixty-five.

THE FORMER
WORLD'S GREATEST
RAW GREEN PEA EATER

He hadn't spoken to her in ten years when he decided to call.

"Hello."

"Miriam?"

"Yes, this is Miriam Cabell, who is it?"

"Miriam Cabell now—I didn't know. What ever happened to Miriam Livin?"

"If you don't mind who is this please?"

"And Miriam Berman?"

"I asked who this is. Now for the last time—"

"Arnie."

"Who?"

"Arnie—well, guess."

"I'm in no good mood for games now, really. And if it's just some crank—well my husband handles all those calls."

"Then Arnie Spear—satisfied, Mrs. Cabell?"

"Arnie Spear? Wait a minute, not Arnie X.Y.Z. Spear?"

"The very same, Madame."

"Arnie Spear the famous sonnet writer and lover of tin lizzies and hopeless causes and the world's greatest raw green pea eater?"

"Well I don't want to brag, but—"

"Oh God, Arnie, how in the world did you get my number?"

"I'm fine, thank you—have a little pain in my ego, perhaps, but how are you?"

"No I'm serious—how'd you get it?"

"I met Gladys Pemkin coming out of a movie the other night. She told me."

"How is Gladys?"

"Fine, I suspect. Haven't you seen her recently?"

"I've been running around so much these days I don't see anyone anymore. In fact, the last time with Gladys must've been a good year ago."

"Your name," he said, "—Cabell? That's your new husband, isn't it?"

"Fairly new. We've been married two years now—or close to two. A lovely man—I wonder if you knew him."

"Don't think so. You happy, Miriam?"

"Happy? Why, was I ever really unhappy? But maybe I should toss this same ticklish nonsense back to you. How about it?"

"I'm happy. Very happy, I suppose. Really doing pretty well these days."

"I'm glad."

"What ever happened to Livin—your last?"

"That bastard? Listen, Arnie, I signed a treaty with myself never to mention his name or even think of him, so help me out, will you?"

"What happens if you break the treaty?"

"What do you mean?"

"I mean if let's say we suddenly begin talking about him. Do you declare war on yourself and sort of battle it out until one or the other side has won?"

"I don't understand. That was a figure of speech. And why would you want to talk about Livin when you never knew him? Anyway, tell me how Gladys looks. Last time I saw her it seemed she'd been drinking it up pretty heavily or at least on pills all day long."

"She seemed fine. A little tired, perhaps, but not much different than the last time I saw her—which was with you, remember?"

"No, when was that?"

"I don't know. About ten years ago or so."

"I can only remember old events if I'm able to place in my mind where I was at the time. Where was I?"

"In this tiny coffee shop on Madison and Fifty-eighth. The Roundtree I think it was called."

"No I don't recall any such place."

"It folded four years ago. I know because for a few months I had a magazine-editing job in the area and used to walk by the shop daily. And then one day it was suddenly empty of everything except a sawhorse and there was a For Rent sign in front. Now it's a beauty shop."

"Wait a minute. Not some incredibly garish beauty shop? With lots of pink and blue wigs on these wood heads in the window and with a refreshment counter in front for serving hot tea and cookies?"

"I think that's the one."

"Do you know, I once went there to have my hair set—isn't that strange? It's not a very good place, which is why I only went once. They dry all your roots out."

"Well that's where we last saw one another. The place has always been particularly meaningful to me—almost as a starting point in a new phase of my life. Because if it wasn't for what you told me there that morning, I doubt whether I ever would've become so immediately conscious of my hang-ups then to flee the city, as I did, and get this fine job out of town."

"Excuse me, Arnie. You're on that beauty shop still?"

"Don't you remember? We met there for coffee—when it was still a coffee shop. It was an extremely emotional scene for me then—holding your hand, and both of us unbelievably serious and me trying to work up enough courage to finally propose to you. You very mercifully cut me off before I was able to make a big ass out of myself and told me, and very perceptively I thought, what a shell of an existence I was leading at the time and how, instead of trying to write fiction about a world I didn't know, I should get a job and see what the world was about. I was so despondent after that—"

"Yes. Now I remember."

"Remember how torn up I was? I was a kid then, granted, but it was very bad, extremely crushing."

"Yes. I hated that last scene."

"So after that, I quit school two days later and got a cub-reporter slot on the Dallas paper my brother was on then, just so I could be away from you and the city and all. And later, I went to Washington for several local Texas papers and then the correspondent jobs overseas seemed to pour in, none of which I feasibly could have taken if I were married or seriously attached at the time."

"Then things have worked out in their own way, right?"

"I suppose you might say so."

"And you've also seen a lot of the world, am I right? I mean, Europe and such?"

"Europe, Central America, Rio and Havana and once even a year's stint in Manila as a stringer for one of the TV networks. I've had a good time."

"I'm glad."

"I've been very fortunate for a guy who never had a thought of going into journalism—very."

"It really sounds like it. There can't be anything more exciting than traveling, I think. Besides the fact of also making money from it."

"Even then, it's not as if I've had everything I exactly wanted—like the wife and kids I always spoke about."

"That's right. You used to speak about them a lot."

"Or the home. The even relatively permanent home with some grounds I could putter around with on weekends, for basically I'm a family and fireplace man and I'd be a self-deluding idiot to deny it. But I've been quite lucky all in all."

"It sounds like it. It sounds very exciting."

"Yes. Then last night, when we were in the lobby waiting for the movie to break—"

"You were with someone?"

"A friend—a woman I see. Nothing important: someone I was serious about long ago. Well I spotted Gladys, and I don't know, I just ran over to her and for some reason threw my arms around her—something I never would've done ten years ago as I had never cared for her much. But things change. I was actually exhilarated at seeing her. And we naturally got around to talking about you."

"What did Gladys have to say about me?"

"Nothing much."

"I ask that because she's always had a foul mouth. Always

spreading lies about people—me particularly, though I was probably the first person to even take a half-interest in her. She's another one I made a pact with myself never to speak to or even think about. She's said some filthy malevolent things about me—to mutual friends, no less, which we'd be cut off the line now if I ever repeated them."

"For me she's always had a special ironic place in my memory. Because if you remember, when we finally emerged from that coffee shop ten years ago, Gladys was walking past—the last person we wanted to see at the time, we agreed when we saw her."

"Now I remember. That bitch always turns up at the wrong moments."

"She spotted us and smiled and began waving an arm laden with clanky chains, as if this was just the most beautiful day in the most beautiful of worlds for everyone in it. I remember her vividly."

"You always had an excellent memory. I suppose that's important in your field."

"That among other things. But that incident comes back amazingly clear. Even the kind of day it was, with the ground freshly covered with a light snow flurry which we had watched from the coffee shop."

"That part," she said, "I'm afraid I don't remember."

"Everyone must have a few scenes in his life which stick out prominently. And not just extraordinary or life-changing events—that's not what I'm driving at so much. For instance, I can remember meaningless, supposedly insignificant incidents which occurred twenty years ago, and also what kind of day it was then and how everyone looked and even what they were wearing down to the pattern of their dresses and ties."

"What was I wearing that day?"

"That day? —Oh . . . that green suit you had. And a trench coat. The tightly belted coat I particularly remember, even that the top button was off and that you said that right after you leave me you were heading straight to a notions shop to get the button replaced."

"That trench coat," she said. "I got it at the British-American House and did it ever cost a fortune, though I at least got a few years out of it. But the green suit?"

"It was a green tweed, salt-and-pepper style. It was a very fashionable suit at the time—the one you most preferred wearing to your auditions."

"Nowadays, I just go in Levis or slacks."

"You usually wore it with the amber-bead necklace I gave you, and so I always felt at least partially responsible for the parts you got."

"I forgot about that necklace. You know I still have it."

"You're kidding."

"I wasn't about to throw it away. It's a nice necklace."

"How does your husband react to your sporting these priceless gems from other men?"

"Mr. Cabell? He doesn't think a thing about my clothes—not like you used to do: nothing. But he's very nice. A very peaceful man who knows where he is more than most anyone, and extremely generous. He's a dentist."

"About my favorite professional group—even if they hurt."

"But he's not like any old dentist. He specializes in capping teeth for theater people. Just about every big Broadway or television-commercial name who's had his or her teeth capped had it done by my husband. That's how I first met him."

"You had your teeth capped?"

"Just the upper front part. Only four of them."

"But you always had such beautiful teeth."

"Well he thought they should be capped. They were a little pointy—the incisors especially—like fangs. They look much better for it—honestly."

"What could a job like that run someone?"

"Thousand plus—which is with a cleaning and everything. But then you have to consider the labor and time involved."

"Did Dr. Cabell make you pay up before he married you?"

"Oh we got married long after that. You see, about six months after I paid up completely, he phoned me out of the blue and mentioned something about my having missed one of my monthly payments. I said 'Oh no, Dr. Cabell, there must be some mistake,' and he said he'd have his nurse check it out. Later he called back and said I was right—I was paid up in full. That's when he first asked me out for lunch—to make up for his misunderstanding, he explained—and later we got married."

"It sounds as if he were initially feeding you a line."

"What do you mean?"

"I mean, quite harmlessly, that he was feeding you a line—which is all right if it works I suppose."

"But that's not true. He in fact told me later that I'd probably think his bill call was only an excuse to contact me, but that it wasn't. He really did think I wasn't paid up."

"Then why didn't he have his nurse phone you about your overdue payment? That would seem both more logical and professional to me, considering how busy dentists always say they are."

"Simon feels that something like that—when he has the time—ought to be handled by him alone. He's a very informal man, Arnie, and he's told me many times that there's already too much impersonality in the city between dentist and patient."

"You're no doubt right. It's absurd for me to even have brought up such a small point. But I suppose I've been hauling around this vision of you being a person who'd be much cleverer than to fall, let's say, for the kind of business like that."

"Fall? What are you talking about? I married this man. Even if he was giving me the business with that call—which he wasn't—what's the difference now? It's all water under the cesspool or something when you married the person, isn't it?"

"Naturally."

"Oh sure, you really sound convinced."

"Look, I'm simply against lines and deceptions of all sorts—what can I tell you? I don't like hypocrisy. I've seen too much of it in my work and I simply don't like it."

"That's right—I forget. You're the big world traveler and interpreter of newsy events."

"All right, I happen to be a journalist—a newsman, if you like. And I write about things that turn my stomach every day. In politics, diplomacy, newspaper management—"

"You were also always a big one for the soapbox if I can remember. Even in college: always the big speech."

"No, you're not catching my point, Miriam."

"Oh I catch it. I haven't been sleeping these past ten years. But one would think that during this time you might have changed. But you still have to beat the old drum."

"I'm not beating any old drum. I was simply saying—"

"And that you might have learned some tact. Because to call up an old friend and insult her husband as if he were the world's worst hypocrite and schemer, well uh-uh, I'm sorry, that's not using much tact. That's not even using much brains, if I can say so without you jumping down my throat."

"I'm not jumping down anyone's throat—especially not yours. I happen to like your throat. I once even loved your throat. I'd never try and hurt you—and I didn't intend to insult your husband. I'm not quite sure I ever did, but let's drop it."

"Why don't we."

There was a long silence before he said "Miriam. Miriam, you still there?"

"Yes. And I really have to go now, Arnie. The baby—"

"You have a baby? When I spoke to Gladys—"

"It's not mine—just the child of a friend in the building. I'll have one though. We're working on it."

"I'm sure you will. And then it's been good speaking to you, Miriam."

"A little rough at times, but I'm glad we can still say it was nice after all."

"Don't be silly. And also—it might sound asinine to suggest we meet for lunch one time this week, but I'll be around that length of time. And it's originally what I called for."

"It's probably not a very good idea right now, so maybe another time."

"A quick coffee then. Just for a half-hour or so, and if not at a shop then perhaps I can even come up to your place. It'd be interesting seeing you again, and then these scenes of ancient college boyfriends popping over after so many years have almost become proverbial in books and movies by now. You know, where the husband just stands aside while these two sort of conspire in their talk about those dreamy goofy college days. And then the husband having a fat laugh about it with his wife when the silly old beau goes."

"I don't think it's a good idea, really. I've never been much for conspiracies. Call up again when I'm less hassled by work and getting a new apartment furnished and I'm sure we can spend some time together. I love talking over old times with good friends."

"So do I."

Then she was gone. He said goodbye, but she didn't hear him: her receiver had already been recradled. He bought a newspaper and walked the fifteen blocks to Penn Station, since he had more than an hour to kill. About ten minutes before his train was scheduled to leave for Philadelphia and his parents and kid sister waiting for him on the platform, all eager to see him after his two years away and planning a big family party tonight to celebrate his return before he went overseas again, he rushed out of the club car and phoned Miriam.

"Hello? Hello? Hello?" she said, and after her fifth hello he hung up.

He called back a short time later and the woman who answered told him in a stiff telephone operator's voice that the party he was dialing was no longer a working number. The next time he phoned it was a thick rolling Bavarian voice that answered, saying "Isolde's Fine German Pastry shop, dis is Isolde speaking, vould you like to place an order?" He said "No, maybe some other time, thanks," and hung up. She always had a sharp ear for dialect. It almost always used to break him up.

MOM IN PRISON

She visits her husband in prison. It's a long train ride up or seemed that way but now looking back she sees it couldn't have been more than an hour and a half, maybe two. The trains were very old, the windows were still open in the hot weather then; the passenger cars were more like very long subway cars going above ground, but between stations not as fast. All that, plus stopping at every stop, probably had something to do with making the trip seem longer. Also that she had to take the subway to Times Square and then the Forty-second Street shuttle to Grand Central to get the train. If it had had a shiny high-speed look to it she might have remembered it as going faster. It also could have been her mood. She never felt good going, always felt worse returning, so she was never able to sleep or read on the train, not even a newspaper. He was awful then: cranky, angry, bitter, inconsiderate, unfeeling. Tough as it was for him to be there, it wasn't so easy for her either. But he never said things to her like "How you holding up? It must be rough, not just this back-and-forth trip, but taking care of the kids and being so short of cash and going along on your own day-to-day. I'm miserable without you too and for what I've done to you, but please don't let that add to your upset; I'll get through it okay." She left the children in the care of someone. All of them except the youngest go to the same elementary school three blocks from their home, so it shouldn't be too tough on the woman. She's allowed to see him once a month for up to two hours,

and every week if she wants, except the one she comes up for
the long visit, for ten minutes. Documentary trips they call those.
Sign this, that's it, out. She's never gone for just those ten minutes. Wants no part of them; so cold. If there's business between
them she saves it for the long visit when they can also talk about
other things. The business stuff can be brutal and it's also a long
trip and so many preparations and expensive for just ten minutes. They're not allowed to touch. Signs say it everywhere, unless the couple is given written permission by the chief guard.
"They might give it if I'm a perfect boy for a year," her husband
once said. "But fingers through the hole only, so expect no kiss."
Glass is between them where they sit. A screened hole the size
of a silver dollar in it to talk through and a hole the size of his
fist at the bottom of it to eventually touch fingertips she hopes
and to put things through for him to sign if she has to. When
that happens a guard unlocks the hole on her side, another guard
stands beside her husband, and the paper and pen, having been
inspected by the chief guard in the anteroom before she comes
into this meeting room, are put through by the guards. Then the
hole's locked, and after he signs, hole's unlocked and the pen and
paper's passed through to her guard who reads it to see her
husband didn't write anything he wasn't supposed to, like, she
supposes, "Put a hand grenade in a cake to help me escape," or
even "I love you dearly and want to screw you madly," and given
to her. Today she wants him to sign a change-of-name form for
the kids. "Where does that leave me?" he says. She says "What
do you mean?" "It means no one will ever know me through my
kids." "It doesn't have to mean that. It could mean we just wanted to make their lives simpler by Anglicizing their names. But
all right, I warned you not to do it, you kept doing it. I warned
you some more, you kept doing it some more and a whole slew
of other stupid things which thank God—don't worry, nobody
can hear me—you were never caught at. I warned and warned
you even more—" "Stop harping on me. Don't be a bitch. You
know I don't like bitches. I never did and you're acting like a
total worthless foulmouthed nagging bitch of all time. It makes
you look ugly when by all rights you could be pretty." "Insults
won't change my mind or the conversation's direction." "Sticks
and stones, go on and tear me to pieces and chew up my bones,

think I care? think I'd dare? blah-blah-blah, you rotten bag. Just lay off." "Stop being a jackass and trying to avoid this. Please sign. That's all I ask. Please, please sign." "Why?" "We've gone over it." "Why?" "It's best for the kids." "How?" "You're like a broken record." "How?" "Because they're being hounded, as I've already told you, hounded by their schoolmates and other people because their father's in prison and lost his dental license and was involved in a smelly citywide scandal and newspaper stories and photos of you and the whole world and his brother knows of it and other things. Because you're famous in the most terrible low way. And through you, guess." "So it'll be better by the time I come out." "The news stories. Think, why don't you. Just don't sit there pigheaded, unconcerned for anyone but you. People will never forget, or not for thirty years. The *Mirror*'s centerfold photo of you on the courthouse steps, for one thing." "What was so wrong with it? I was dressed well, looked good, big smile, wasn't in cuffs." "The lousy change, nickels and dimes, falling through your pants pocket and rolling down the steps and you chasing after it like a snorting hog." "What's the snorting? What's with these pigs?" "Panting. You were out of shape. But for the money, is what I mean. The same kind of man running after petty change where he could break his neck or get a stroke would try to save a few dollars in fines by bribing a building inspector. Whatever it is, that's why they took it and used it and it was ugly." "I told you to sew those holes." "That's hardly my point. Besides, you cram so much change and keys in them, your pockets are always going to have holes." "I need the change for the bus and subway. And newspapers." "Since when do you buy your own newspaper?" "I buy it." "Maybe for Sundays. The rest you take out of garbage cans." "Sometimes if it's a clean one and just laying there on top, but obviously clean and looking almost unread, why not? Why waste? So many people waste. I was brought up poor and taught not to." "Sometimes some of the ones you brought home had spit on them and, once, dog doody." "I didn't see. The subway station was poorly lit or something. But one out of a hundred. So what?" "Let's drop the subject and concentrate on the other one." "What other one?" "Three people have already sent that photo to me through the mail. All anonymously. What did you do to make so many enemies? Anyway, it's an example of how many people know about it regarding the children." "I didn't make enemies. If I made a lot more money than most other dentists, maybe that's why. Jealousy, and this is how they get even with me, but behind my back. Or there are thousands of crazy people in the city who do nothing all day but read the papers. And when they see a man down, someone they've never even laid eyes on but through the papers think they know, they get their kicks pushing him further. But believe me, people will forget. In a year, two at the most. I'll be old news, or their minds just don't remember that far. The few who don't forget, the hell with them. I'll tell all those nut jobs and sickies that I did it standing on one foot." "What do you mean?" "That it was easy—this is—and in some ways, even good for me. I've met lots of decent people here. Gentlemen. Men of means. Big successes in all kinds of fields. Future clients, some of them. They have me working in the prison clinic." "I know." "So, for one thing, I'm able to stay in touch with the latest dental gadgets and machines. It's very well-equipped. But best yet, I see twenty patients a day, all men from the prison. No thieves or killers but tax evaders, embezzlers, extortionists, but not strong-armed ones, plus some draft dodgers. Those I don't especially like, for what they're doing, but that's their business. And the conscientious ones who won't go into the army for their own more personal reasons. Moral, religious, none of which I go along with or else don't understand, but at least they're better types. And they all got teeth. Most, I just look in their mouths, pick around a little and take an X-ray or two to satisfy them, since they usually have nothing wrong with them a quick prison release wouldn't cure or else need major bridgework, some of them complete upper and lower plates, which the prison's not going to put out for. They let me extract and fill and even do root canal on as many teeth as I want, since they don't want their inmates walking around in pain and maybe kicking someone over it. But they feel the more expensive work, which means sending it out to a dental lab, the prisoner should pay for himself on the outside. All of which is to the good, since when a lot of these men get out they'll come to me." "How? You won't have a license to practice when you get out." "I'll get it in a year, maybe two." "You might get it in ten years if you're lucky. That's what I've been told." "By who?" "The license people and Democratic club leaders you sent me to speak to for you." "Don't worry, I'll get it much sooner. But till I do I'll get different kind of work and do very well in it. I did in dentistry—started with borrowed money and no more skills than the next dentist—I can do well in other things. And by working at it long and hard and mixing in the right places a lot. I bought a house for us from it, didn't I? A building. Five stories of it and you decorated it to your heart's content." "Fine. One where it cost more to keep up than the rents we get plus all the problems that go along with it." "What problems? Be like me. Tenant complains, tell him to move out if he doesn't like it. And we also got our apartment from it. Two floors. And my office, so those were supposed to make up the difference. And it was an investment if the neighborhood ever turned good. Not only that, we had other things. A full-time maid. One left, another came the next day. And a car whenever we needed one. And summer vacations for all of us but especially all summer for you and the kids. So stop complaining. I can do all that again no matter what I go into. And maybe a little dentistry—the hell with them—you know," and he makes jabbing motions with his thumb over his shoulder, indicating he'll do it on the side or behind their backs. "Till everything comes through." "That's exactly what you shouldn't do. They'll find out—one of your good friends who's an enemy will squeal—and you'll land right back here getting acquainted with all the latest dental instruments." "Anyway, no job is that complicated unless it's a real profession like dentistry and medicine and law. But I'm sure I won't have to do anything else for very long. The people you spoke to were being extra-cautious. You're my wife. How do they know you weren't also working for the state, in return for helping to reduce my sentence or getting my license back, by letting them say, 'Well now, you want him to get his license back sooner than ten years, you'll have to pay for it.' They're no dopes. I never should have sent you to them, but thanks for trying. Because of course they built up the time to you till I get my license back and pretended to be saints. But when I see them I'll talk to them like a boy from the boys. And on a park bench—no one in fifty feet of us or where the air can be bugged—and not in a restaurant or room. I know what to do." "What? Bribing them?" "Shut your mouth. That one they heard. Say something quick and silly as if you were joking." "They didn't hear. And like how," she whispers, "by bribing them?" "Shut up with that word. I'm serious. Smile. Make believe you're laughing, the whole thing a joke." She smiles, throws her head back, closes her eyes, opens her mouth wide and goes "huh-huh-huh" through it. "Okay," her face serious again, "what'll you do? The same stupid thing?" "That time was a mistake. I did it to the wrong inspector." "He was a city investigator, not a building inspector." "I thought different. He was an impersonator, that's what he was—a lowlife mocky bastard in it for a promotion or raise. Or maybe he does both—inspects, investigates—when there's cause for alarm or just that things are getting too hot in the department that other inspectors are taking graft. So one true-blue one in there. But they all take, so they wouldn't use an inspector to investigate." "You did it to all the inspectors. Fire, water, boiler, sewage—whatever they were, that was your philosophy in owning a building. Even if I'd seen to every inch of the building and complied to the last decimal to every city rule and law, matter of course you handed out fives and tens to them." "To keep them happy. They expect it. They don't get it they feel unhappy and can write out ten violations at a single inspection, some that'll cost hundreds to correct. Or my office. I got water and electricity and intricate machine equipment I depend on and I don't want them closing me down even for a day. Every landlord knows that and every professional man who owns and works in his own building." "It's a bad way to run a brownstone, and dishonest." "But it's the practical way, or was. Did we ever get a violation before? Why do you think why? They're all on the take or were till the investigation, and probably now are again. There's a lull, then it's hot; it never stops. Cities are run on it, the mayor on down. What happened then was they were using me. They wanted to get a professional man bribing an investigator impersonating an inspector so they could say 'See, even doctors and dentists give bribes, so how bad is it that our building inspectors take them? Dentists earn five times as much as our inspectors and get from the public ten times the respect, but the briber is as serious a criminal as the bribee,' or whatever they call them the bribed guy who takes. And that's why they trapped me and that doctor in Staten Island and the

C.P.A. who owns a much bigger building—an apartment one, twelve stories—in the Bronx. I met them both, since they're both here for around the same-length terms as mine. Nice family men and they shouldn't be in prison. For what good does it? You want to make them pay, have them work in city clinics or helping the poor with their taxes for twenty hours a week for the next few years. Ten hours, but where it adds up to about what they'd put in nonsleeping time here." "Please sign the name change." "I can't. I know you think it's best for them, that it's going to help their future. But today's big graft and news story will be tomorrow's trash, or something—yesterday's news. Last year's. Last two. That's what I wanted to say. No one will even have heard of the case or remembered my name from it by then. 'Doc who? Nah, what graft story's in the paper today?' And I'll be out and practicing again with an even bigger clientele. And if I'm not? If they're so stupid to deprive my family of a good livelihood and the country of a lot more income taxes because of some dumb bribe I gave a dumb building inspector or investigator or actor, then I'll do something else. The Garment Center. I'll sell dresses or sweaters or materials. One fine gentleman in here on some illegal—immigration or something—offense owns a large suit-and-cloak house on Thirty-fifth Street and says he'll take me in as a salesman the minute I get out. If he's still in here, he'll tell his partner to put me on. Not road-selling but the showroom. He thinks I'm sharp and palsy-walsy, so just the right type, besides knowing my way around and eager for money. And it'll give the house a little extra class, having a doctor working for them. They all wanted to be doctors or dentists or their parents wanted them to. Most of the men here bullshit, so you can't really count on them. But I know lots of people in the Garment Center, and also one of the ones from here might come through. And in it for a couple of years, working very hard, I'll eventually learn enough to start my own business. I can do all that, why not? And then we'll be rolling again. But to have my kids walking around with the name Teller when I'm Tetch? How am I to explain it?" "You don't have to." "No, I do. 'Meet my son Gerald Teller'? 'Was your wife married before and the boy kept his real father's name?' 'No, I'm his real father. Same blood and nose.' 'Then why the different names?' 'Because all the kids want to be bank tellers when they grow up and my wife thought it'd give them a head start.'" "That's just stupid," she says. "Why, you got a better explanation? Okay. 'Because I was in prison for being too honest and my wife thought to really jab the knife in me to get even she'd change the kids' name so no one would know they were mine.' Because you don't think that's what people will ask? Over and over they will. For what father has a different name than his kids?" "People we know are always shortening or Anglicizing their names. But if you don't like that one, I was thinking of another. Tibbert. It sounded good." "It sounds awful. It has no meaning. It sounds like a bird or frog or some little barnyard animal singing by a brook or up a tree. 'Tib-bert! Tib-bert!' Anyway, something silly sitting on a lily pad in a pond. Look, don't give me that paper. You do, don't give me the pen, because I won't take both at the same time. I won't be pressured. Just because I'm here, I haven't become a jellyfish." "I'll tell you what you've become." "Sure, and you're my wife. But what about Tibbs as a name? We'll start shortening the Anglicized. Or Tubbs? Or Terbert? We can change Howard's name to Herbert and he'll be Herbert Terbert. Or forget the T. Who says in a name change it has to start with the same letter as Tetch? Sherbet. Gerald, Alex, Howard and Vera Sherbet. The Sherbet kids. They can go on stage. Tell jokes, take off their clothes, do little two-steps. I don't know why, but it sounds all right. Or the Shining Sherbets. Up on the high wire. You can change your name to Sherbet too and go back on the stage or up there in the air with them. You still got the face and figure for it. Or just divorce me if you want." "Oh please." "I'm not kidding. You want it, you got it." "What are you talking about? Though don't think for a few moments I haven't thought of it." "So think of it some more, think of it plenty. What the hell do I care anymore? You're so ashamed of me—" "It's not that—" "You're ashamed!" "Well I told you not to do—" "You told me and you told me and now I'm here doing it on one foot and soon I'll be out on both, or not so soon but a lot sooner than any of my kids' lifetimes so far and later everything will be forgotten and the same. Except I probably won't be doing those things again, that's for sure, but you'll still be hocking me about it till I'm dead. In fact your hocking will make me dead. Look, you want a divorce, it's yours, on a platter.

Take the house, the kids, the platter and whatever you find in the mattresses. You find another kid there, take that one along too." "Don't give me what I don't want. When you get out and if you still want it, we'll talk. The children will be a little older then and maybe more able to adjust to it. But not now." "Why not now? Why not? Why not?" The guard on her side comes over. "Anything the matter?" "Nothing's the matter, thank you." "She says nothing but let me tell you what she wants me to do," tapping the glass to the paper on the table in front of her. "He knows, they all have to know. It had to be screened before it got to you." "So good, everyone knows. But did you know," he says to the guard, "she wants to force me to do it? She thinks I'll bend, because prison somehow has weakened me, but not me, sir, not me." "Please, Simon, let it ride," she says. "Okay, it'll ride, to please you. Everything to please you, except that goddamn name change." "Let that ride too." "I'm afraid to say your time's about up," the guard says to them. "That's what I really came over to say." "Okay, okay, thanks, but just a few seconds more. —How's the new dentist doing in the office?" he says to her. "Better than the last. He seems to be busy, mostly older people—plates, extractions, primarily, from talking to a few of them going in and out." "Just like me then. I pull out about ten teeth a day here and does it ever feel good. And some of these guys are *bulvon*, with teeth like dinosaurs'. —I'll pull out yours too, Mr. Carey, if you want me to—no charge." "Thanks but no. Ones I don't need I let fall out." "Smart guy. And I know you're Carey because you got it stitched on your jacket. Don't let me fool you." "You didn't." "But no plates here," he says to her. "They won't shoot for it for the prisoners. But I already said that. I'm repeating myself when I've only got seconds left. I'd like to be making them. Keep my hands in so I don't get rusty. Does he pay the rent on time?" "First of the month. And for the summer, when he was going to a dental convention in Chicago and then on to a vacation somewhere—Denver, he said; the Grand Canyon to hike and ride horses—" "Lucky guy. Not the hiking, but I used to ride horses. Once in army training, then in Prospect Park a couple of times. I've pictures. You've seem them." "—he gave me two months in advance. I think he'll be there for as long as we like." "Tell him not to get too tied to the place. Or why not? I'll open an office

someplace else. It doesn't always have to be in my own home."
"Time's really up," Carey says. "Now we're all breaking rules and
can be penalized. Your wife, with shortening her visits. You, because of that. Me, in that they don't like me being this lenient
at the end of a visit and I get a talking-to—" "Can I kiss her
hand through the bottom hole here?" "Afraid not." "Right now
she wouldn't go for it anyway." He stands. "Goodbye, dear," she
says. "I mean it: please call and write as often as you can. And
try to forget most of what we went over today—what might
disturb you." "The kids. Give them each a big kiss on the head
from me." Carey signals a guard behind the glass, who goes over
to her husband. "Tell them I love them like nobody does but don't
tell them where I am." Carey shuts the speaking hole. "Gerald
knows." Her husband cups his hand to his ear and his expression
says "What?" "I don't want to get you in trouble here," she says
louder, "but Gerald knows." "Yeah, I know, I know," he shouts,
"but not the others and tell Gerald not to tell." Carey opens the
hole and says "Everything all right, Yitzik?" Yitzik waves that
everything's fine, puts his hand on her husband's shoulder and
says "Please don't make a fuss." "Me? A fuss? You hear that,
Pauline? This nice guard here thinks I'm going to make a fuss.
—Not good-time Simon, sir. Not a chance," and without looking
at her or back at her he goes with the guard through a door.
She puts the paper back into a manila envelope, winds the string
around the tab in back to close it, goes through her door, is asked
if anything was slipped to her by the prisoner and is given her
pocketbook back, calls for a cab, leaves the prison, takes the cab
to town, goes to a bar near the train station and has two strong
drinks, something she only started doing every day once he went
to prison and which she has one or two more of and never has
supper or lunch the day she visits him.

WRONG WORDS

"So we've come right down to this," I say.

"Right down to it," she says.

"Then I'm going."

"Please do."

"You were always so polite."

"Please isn't a dirty word, as we used to say."

"We used to say 'is not, is not.' Anyway, I'm on my way."

I try opening the door.

"The door's locked," I say.

"Unlock it."

"I mean the fucking catch in the middle of the damn lock's jammed."

"You know I don't like the word damn."

"The epithet, don't you mean?"

"The expletive's more like it."

"Expletive is really what I meant instead of epithet."

"Though it could also be epithet, I think. I'm sorry. I'm not sure."

"You don't mean 'not quite sure'?"

"Just not sure."

"But expletive we're both quite or just sure about, correct?"

"At least I am."

"Then the expletive damn."

"No, epithet I think is more precise."

"One or the other: make up your mind."

"I don't think my choice has to be as decisive as that."

"I'm sure you meant definitive then."

"What I meant was that there are other synonyms for the words expletive and epithet. Oath, for instance."

"Oath, indeed," I say.

"I meant for the word expletive or epithet—the noun."

"Expletive or epithet can also be adjectives or exclamations."

"Damn can, not expletive, oath or epithet. And I'm not even sure if damn can be an adjective. But foul invective's another nounal synonym I'm thinking of for oath. And cuss word, sailor's blessing—plenty of them. Profanity also comes to mind."

"My dear."

"To me now that sounds like a profanity—your 'my dear.'"

"I was only being satirical. No, satirical isn't the word."

"You're not thinking of ironic?"

"Caricatural—that's the word."

"Of who?"

"If caricatural's the right word."

"Even if it isn't, who were you being it of?"

"Ridiculous is the word," I say. "Though not quite ridiculous, but ridiculing. Though that doesn't sound like the right word either. Help me. What's the word I was being of people before?"

"Which people? That was my question before in slightly different words."

"You mean 'what people,' though actually either of our terms could work. But I meant of people who say damn is a profane word. With that certain pinch-nosed, upper-crust, highfalutin accent. You know—the 'my dear' kind of people. 'Fancy that, my dear. Nasty weather out, my dear.'"

"Oh, nasty weather in?"

"Nasty weather outside, I meant. But out is acceptable."

"Inacceptable."

"Unacceptable."

"Out isn't acceptable for the word outside. You either say 'nasty weather outside' or just 'nasty weather.' If the people you're saying either of these to are inside or outside, they'll know what you mean when you say 'nasty weather,' as the weather can't be nasty inside unless there's a huge hole in the roof or no roof. And if there is no roof or a very big hole in the roof, then I'm sure their main concern wouldn't be the nasty weather but in getting that roof repaired and possibly a place to sleep that night or for as many nights as it takes to get that roof repaired."

"I was saying those expressions with the 'my dear' in them before like a person I'm not—that's all."

"'As a person I'm not.'"

"No, you're wrong on that. Absolutely. Maybe I was saying 'my dear' such as a person I'm not, but definitely not as a person I'm not."

"Absolutely? Definitely?"

"Almost absolutely or definitely."

"Well I think you're wrong," she says.

"You're quite sure, my dear?"

"Quite."

"Like a person like that. That's all I meant. Like someone who uses the word quite just like you just did."

"You mean 'such as a person such as' or 'as a person such as' or 'such as a person as that.'"

"Sure about all that?"

"Not quite sure. Not at all. But you were going, did I hear you say?"

"You did. I was going when I found the door was locked. Not locked, I later found, but the hold-and-release catch in the lock was jammed."

"You also found the door, am I right?"

"I didn't have to find the door. Standing anywhere in your house I know instinctively where's the door."

"You mean 'where the door is'?"

"I know instinctively where your door is, yes."

"And 'instinctively.' You don't mean 'intuitively' perhaps?"

"Intuitively and automatically and the rest of those and you be fucking damned let me add."

"You know I don't like the profanity damn."

"I said damned."

"That too."

"Not 'that also'?"

"Also or too, either one. You know what I don't like though."

"I know quite well what you don't like, my dear, and I couldn't give a goddamn."

"Please go," she says.

"Nor do I like or appreciate your pleases. They don't mean anything."

"Then just go."

"That's better. But your hold-and-release catch, if it is called that, in your rim lock, and I'm sure it's called that, is jammed and the door won't open."

"Then try and fix it."

"I can't fix it. And if you can't fix it or find some way to release that catch immediately, I'm going to kick down your door."

"If that's the quickest way to get you out of here, then please do."

"I please will."

"Will you please go?"

I kick the door lock with my heel a few times. The catch spring breaks and the door swings open.

"I'm leaving," I say.

"Good riddance."

"You don't mean 'goodbye'?"

"I mean good riddance and goodbye and all the other vale-dictums, leave-partings and fare-thee-wells."

"You don't mean valedictions and farewells?"

"I meant and mean them all. Goodbye, good riddance, good-night forever, ex-partner, and if I never see you again may that be time enough."

"You don't mean 'If I never see you again may that be soon enough'?"

"I mean something like that and much more."

"Well, you know—and I think I can say that 'you know' even if I don't think I've ever said this to you before—I'm kind of glad to be rid of you too."

"You haven't quite rid yourself of me yet."

"Once I leave this house, I mean."

"The feeling's mutual."

"That's what I meant."

She turns her back to me.

"You've nothing more to say?" I say.

She shuts the door.

"Your door can't lock," I say. "I said your door can't lock.

Your door doesn't lock. You'll have to get the door fixed if you want it to lock. I mean, the door lock fixed if you want the lock to lock. Or just another rim lock put on, which means your door fixed if you want your door to lock. Or if I kicked your door too hard when I broke the lock and by doing so also broke your door, then both your door and lock fixed if you want your door with this lock to lock."

She throws open the door and comes at me with a candlestick. Not "comes at me," but races toward me with the candlestick. Not "races toward me," but it's too late as the candlestick comes down on my head. Not "comes down," but came down and maybe the candlestick came down on my head many times or came many times down on my head or just came down many times on my head, for when I did come to or out of it or out of unconsciousness as it can also be said, I was on a bed in a hospital room, a bandage around my head. And I was trying to remember, so I could make sure I still had the power or ability or facility or faculty or capacity or capability or whatever it is of memory, what it was or why or how I got to this hospital in the first place. What it was about me that was instrumental or whatever the word is that helped bring me here, just so I won't do it again.

THE DOCTOR

The nurse. She bathes and dries me. Shaves me and dresses me in my very best. My suit. My white shirt and even has my shoes shined. But she doesn't know how to make a tie right. That's okay. "Just tie it a little tighter at the knot," I say. She does. "Not so tight," I say, "or they'll get you for choking me to death and not for letting me expire in a more proper medical way." She laughs. They like me here. Doctor Sweet Guy I've been nicknamed. That's okay. Undignified expression maybe, but something I've gotten to like. I'd maybe like anything today because it's my third day out of intensive care and a Sunday. And on Sundays everybody has visitors and no matter how many times I've said nobody has to visit me if they got anything else they want to do that day, I'm glad I'm in a room where I can have all I want. My son. My daughter, who's bringing my wife. My sister who lives two blocks away even, though with her who knows? "Two blocks can be the last mile for me," she said over the phone yesterday. My former longtime patients who some of them I'd really be happy to see.

They sit me up in a chair. No bed today. "Thank you very much," I say. "You look very nice," the nurse says. "Thank you very much again and you do too." "You've never seen me in my best clothes," she says, "but maybe one day." "Oh yeah," I say, "maybe one day you and me we'll go dancing at a doctors' convention, okay?" "Okay," she says. She combs my hair. "You got the part wrong I'm afraid." "Sorry," she says and she combs the part on the other side. I'm not supposed to do any of these things by myself just yet. Eating, yes, and answering the phone, but the doctors say nothing else and I'll agree with that. Today it's just cosmetic. I might just look good and as if I did everything myself, but inside I'm still not so hot. She even combs down my mustache. My professional mustache I grew to look older because in those days nobody wanted to go to young doctors, and which fifty years I've never shaved off once. She holds up the mirror to me and says "Nice." I look. I look okay. Like somebody my age who's been in a hospital for two weeks after a fairly serious heart attack, but okay. "Thank you," I say. "Have a nice day," she says, "and if you need anything, just ring." "Thank you very much. You've been very competent and kind." She leaves. I wait.

No one comes. Hours pass. The lady with my lunch and who later takes the tray away, but nobody else. I had to get a private room? They made me get one. "Dad," Alba said, "between you and your medical insurance you can well afford it, and you deserve the best." But I like the idea of talking to other patients and listening to their visitors' conversations and jokes. Laughing and people with feet walking around. People with behinds sitting up and down. "Oh, they'll just bother you," Alba said, "asking you a lot of free doctor and health questions till you never get any rest," even though I wouldn't mind and with all the doctors coming in to see their patients, it would in fact help me to keep in touch. Finally: "It doesn't look right," Alba said, "a doctor should have his own room." But she has too big a mouth. Ordering me. Ordering her mother, who's staying with her till I get out of here and isn't well herself. First Merry got a stroke and when I'm taking care of her at home a year after she comes out of the hospital, I get one too. But hers was much worse and left one side of her partially paralyzed and her mind a little slow and forgetful when it was always so quick and retentive before, so she'll never recover as much as I hope to. And my sister, though with all her illnesses, she has a good excuse. And my longtime patients, though most of them have no cars and live too far away. And of course my son. What's he doing that's so important where he can't visit me today and for the last week or at least call to explain why? But don't get so excited. The doctors here won't even let me read my medical journals for fear I'll get too excited reading them. And there's still plenty of time for visitors to come. Just sit here and sit tight. That same nurse from before stops in the corridor and says "How's it going, doctor?"

"Fine, thank you. I'm feeling just fine."

"Good."

An hour later my phone rings.

"Dad," Alba says, "we won't be able to come see you today. I'm sorry."

"That's too bad. Anything wrong?"

"We were all set to leave with Mom when our neighbor gave Louis four of the best Garden seats for the Harlem Globetrotters game. We didn't want to go, but the boys put up such a holler that we had to give in."

"If you'll be in New York, why don't you drop your mother off here and go to your game and later come back across the bridge again to pick her up?"

"It'd be too much for everyone. All that traveling and traffic on Sunday and bridges four times, and the boys would be exhausted."

"Then leave Louis and the boys at the Garden and you drive here with your mother and later pick them up."

"But I've never seen the Globetrotters. For thirty years I've wanted to see them do their antics and tricky things with the ball and all and I know this will be my only chance."

"Actually, I don't know why I'm making a fuss. I've already told all of you that if you have better things to do, do them instead of coming here. Though I did want to see your mother."

"I know. And both Mom and Louis and I want to see you. We'll come another day. Next weekend. But next weekend you'll be leaving there. So we'll see you when we pick you up and drive you and Mom home."

"Good enough. Let me speak to her please."

"I don't think she's in the best of moods to talk to you right now. That's another reason we didn't want to bring her in. She seems very depressed. I don't know what from. We've given her everything here, treated her royally. Maybe it's not seeing you. Or the boys could be making too much noise, but she'll be fine soon. We're having a friend stay with her while we're in the city. Which is also why we can't get to the hospital. Our friend can only stay so long."

"I understand. But there's nothing wrong or changed with your mother's physical health, is there?"

"No no, I'm not holding anything back. She's the same, don't worry—just depressed. You know how she sometimes gets. I just don't want her to upset you, that's why I don't want to put her on."

"Just let her say hello."

"No, Dad, really. She might cry or break down."

"Okay. Give her my love."

"He gives you his love, Mom."

"Give him my love back," I hear Merry say.

"She says to give you her—"

"I heard, Alba. Thanks."

"Then all right. We'll see you next week. Though I'll call lots before then and Mom will speak to you and maybe the boys. And you're feeling much better?"

"Now that I'm out of intensive care, much."

"Great. Bye, Dad."

Maybe my son will come. But he really is a busy man. I shouldn't be unfair and forget that. Much busier than I ever was and with a lot more pressures. He's a doctor too. He's been phoning in every day on my case my doctor here says, and the doctor says Rom really knows his stuff. When I get discharged Rom's going to make me close my office. Only open three half-days as it is, but he's probably right. I'll just go to the hospital twice a week as I've been doing and continue my medical work there. Seeing how the people are in the geriatric wards. Taking their pulse. Mostly cheering them up and telling them they're going to live long lives. All that new research and drugs and equipment is just too much for me to learn about now. Rom is a specialist though. Much different than me in every way. High liver. Three wives and working on a fourth. Kids from each one also, though we only see the two from the first. Money he makes tons of, but he needs it with his court settlements and office and apartment and vacations and homes here and there and cars and now a boat. He complains about me. His actual words are that I've money up my ass and I'll die with it stuck up there while he never will. He should know better. About my money and that I don't like to curse or hear the words. I have a little money put away for Merry and me and that's all. Just enough in case I'm forced to retire not only from the office but the little I make at the hospital too. In the beginning it was mostly chickens and things and a few dollars I took in. Meat, cheeses, fight passes and cases of beer. But I don't operate. I don't live big. I'm a general man. I examine people, fix little things and try to prevent worse things from happening, make out prescriptions or recommend my patients to higher men. Our big luxury was the car for my house calls and hospital work and a week's vacation in a small Connecticut beach resort twice a year. We lived sort of frugally and always will. What does he mean money up my ass? Lost a little in stocks. Sending him through schools and helping him start his practice took a big bite. And Alba all the way with her degrees and paying off her first husband and every summer her children's summer camps. So I don't have a lot. Some doctors don't. Rom says I lie to him on that. I tell him I'm not. He laughs, says "Listen, I understand. No doctors likes to say how much he's really worth. Somebody wanting a tax informer's cut might get wind of it and then you've lost most of what you've stored up." But he does well. Good for him. And also does teaching work. And maybe he'll come. Or his first ex-wife. Or his oldest child who's now old enough. Or my sister. Or my sisters-in-law and their husbands. Or my brother in New Mexico who hasn't called or sent a card. Or someone. An ex-receptionist of mine or patient I haven't seen in years. Who knows? Word gets around.

"Nurse," I say. It's night. I must have dozed off. My dinner tray is on the table next to my bed. They must have thought I wanted to sleep. "Nurse," I say when she passes my door again.

"Yes?"

"Could you undress me and give me my bedpan and then get me into bed?"

"Certainly, Doctor. Have a nice Sunday?"

"To be honest, I was a little disappointed."

"What happened? Nobody come and visit you?"

"No, my family's all right. Just little things. But I'll be okay. Thank you very much."

HEADS

There were two heads. I don't know. Let me repeat. There were these two heads. I mean two heads. I don't know. I know I don't like going into it, two heads, just two heads, like that, in the grass, in the park. The grass of the park. The small park called Four Corners Park in the center of the city. A poor section of the city where I live, and a park where I always pass on my way to work every clement workday. A small square park about four blocks square. Square park, in the grass, grass almost over the heads of these heads, over their hair. I saw them. There we are. Saw their hair. Hair of these heads, just two heads, nothing else, maybe necks. I didn't see those. But no shoulders. Though there could have been. I didn't stay around to look. But I don't think anything but heads.

This woman comes in. She says "Two heads." I say "What?" "Two heads," she says. I say "What do you mean two heads?" "Two heads," she says. "I'm saying two heads what?" "Just two heads." "Just two heads," I say, "right." "That's right," she says, "two heads." "I know: two heads," I say. "No you don't know," she says. "More than two heads?" "No, more than two heads." "Excuse me, but what else: two necks?" "No," she says. "You saying no meaning no there aren't or weren't more than two heads?" "No," she says, "just two heads." "That's what I said I said," I say. "Two heads: right?" "Right," she says. "No two bodies or two necks on the heads, right?" "Right," she says. "Right," I say. "Right," she says. "Where?" I say.

Coburn told us to check it out. We drove over to the address. Not really an address. One of the four corners of Four Corners Park. We looked. Found nothing. No two heads or one head or body or even a pinky finger of a body was there. Well, maybe there was a finger there. We didn't comb the place out. We looked, that's all. But nothing, at least not in the part of the park the lady told the station they'd be. So we called in. "Coburn," Coburn said. "Coburn, Pretty Boy Josephus here. That Four Corners spot was Sixth and Bridge, check?" "I knew it was another wild goose chase," Coburn said. "Think she could mean someplace else?" I said. "Like where?" "Like another park?" "Let me ask." "She still there?" "You hold on," he said. He came back. "She said definitely Four Corners Park as there can't be another park she can walk to on her way to work on clear days, but possibly another corner of it. She says she was that scared when she saw them and so isn't so sure now." "Maybe you ought to send her out here," I said. "You holding where you are?" "We think we'll try Sixth and River as long as we did Bridge." "I'll send her first thing," he said. "Her coming was of course what we should have done right off, you know." "You telling me my job, Smarty-brains?" "Just thinking out loud," I said, "thinking out loud."

I like vegetables that grow in the park. I don't want to make a big deal of it, but wild fruits and vegetables that grow wild by themselves and don't need any help from anyone like ourselves. More than dandelions, wild onions, tubular things—whatever they're called. I'm not an expert. Just knew a woman once who during our long walks during the war a long time ago showed me these things and said what a waste. So every day now, more than not having anything to do, I go out finding these things, even in winter if there's a touch of spring. To all the nearby parks and sometimes by thumb or bus to the faraway ones or greenbelt around the city if I want to store up. And I'm in this one, in the park I most go to as it's the one closest to home, collecting in my little shopping bag what the park's got to give for nothing and nobody still yet seems to want. Actually an average-sized shopping bag, not one as small for new shoes in a shoe box the shoe stores seem to give or one of the giant bags the department stores use, when two police cars pull up on the park's pedestrian paths on both sides of me at the same time. I put up my hands and drop my shopping bag or to be more exact drop the bag first and put up my hands when all four cops jump out of their cars with their guns undrawn and no sight of a billy seen and I say "I didn't do anything wrong. Just looking for free produce," I say. "What grows wild and free in the grass and falls without my shakes from the trees. That's what I like. Mints, ginkgo drupes, all kinds of herbs and chicory roots to mash up and mix in with my regular coffee grounds to cut down the costs, as I'm poor, so it helps, economically for me, nutritionally, even cathartically too." Jawing on like that. Anything for an excuse. "I'm old. As you can see: in not very hot health." As I don't want to rot in the clink. For along with the woman they're with they're eying me as if still seriously considering arresting me for stealing what's city-owned and all, which I'd well understand for them. That's their job. I mean I could see where they might have a right to pull me in as there are all sorts of ordinances for everything, I suppose, so I'd think surely one for uprooting city property in a public park even if to most people they're just weeds. But one of them says "Put your hands down, get your bag and beat it." So I go.

I said to her "You sure you didn't see what you think you saw on this corner or the corner of Bridge and Sixth or what?" and she said "I'm not certain for sure now, sir, all I know is I saw them, two heads." I said "Well, which is the way you normally walk to work from home?" and she said "That's a good way to approach it, beginning the way I walk to work. I usually walk never through this way but one of the other ways, either around the outskirts of the park going right when I reach the park's entrance at Fourth and River, or straight through it meaning cutting through the park's middle path straight down it like I'm cutting the park in half till I get to Sixth and Bridge. But never this way going left along River past Fifth to Sixth Street and then down to Bridge, never once, don't ask me why. It's no doubt the same distance going first left instead of right, but to me in my mind it seems longer. And I only do go first right around it when I've an extra few minutes or two to kill and I don't want to just cut straight through or when the middle path's suspicious-looking with people, even when I'm in a hurry or late for work, which is usually why I cut straight through though also at times to hear the sounds and smell the trees." "What do you say we try the two corners we haven't tried yet?" I said and the other three nodded as if to say "What do we have to lose as nothing's going to turn up?" and she said "Maybe it is one of those other two. Could be. I at least passed them before. But not here's where I saw those two heads, no sirs. I mean, officers."

I'd seen two things in the grass that looked funny. They looked like human heads. Sticking out of the grass. As if growing out of it. I couldn't believe it. My eyes again, I thought. At first I was startled. Then skeptical of my vision and then I really couldn't believe it when I looked again and thought I saw the same thing. Glasses, I should repair my glasses. Get them repaired I mean. Then walked toward them. An optical illusion of some kind, I was convinced, or whatever those things are in the desert that look like one thing but aren't anything, but sure as breathing my eyes playing tricks. Or nature playing tricks. That's what they are in the desert: both nature and your eyes playing tricks together or on one another at one time. Or just rocks looking like heads. That's more likely. This was no desert. But I was wrong. They were heads. I got my own head down close enough to lick them. A man and a woman. On the ground, tucked in the grass. Not easy to detect. Maybe easier for someone with better eyes. But up close easy enough to detect. Looking like two people buried up to their necks. Rather one of them up to his chin, the woman up to her neck. It was a horrible sight. I don't see how I can say that so dispassionately. Passively, I mean. One of those two words. Maybe another. But how can I think about words when I talk of those heads? That's because it happened before. How the human bean does forget. Half an hour ago or more. But there they were. And I'll tell you: still pretty much there now in my head. Woman with her eyes open, man's eyes closed. This I'll never forget: both facing one another, lips close enough to kiss. I'd even call it a kiss. Someone had put them there as a joke. When this someone had set up the heads I mean, for certainly decapitating, and that's the word, two heads, is no joke. I thought: must get the police. Thought: I really should yell my fool head off for help. Thought: now there's one accidental joke of my own. Thought: those poor people, these poor heads. For I really didn't know what they were, what name to give them.

Were they married, man and wife? Brother and sister then? Not married, brother and sister, or just friend and friend? Strangers to one another till they met if they ever did meet? Thought: enemies? Maybe enemy and friend. Poor heads. Where were their spirits now? Underground? Circling around my knees? Floating away? Already there if there's a there? All that's what I thought then. Or maybe the spirits were still in these heads. Does it take them five minutes to go, ten? But even if I knew how long it takes spirits to go, I'd also, to know if they were gone, have to know how long these heads have been here. But these poor people or heads. Still my thoughts from before. In the grass just sitting there. Sitting heads. Like sitting ducks. That made no sense then and doesn't now. A boy came over. "What you looking at, mister?" I said "Go away." He said "Why, you find anything valuable?" I said "It's something I don't want you looking at, so go away." "I don't want to go away. What is it?" "You want to be useful to me, call the police." "Call them for what?" "For something you don't want to see in the grass." "What's in the grass?" "Something you don't want to see." "And what's that?" "How old are you?" "Sixteen." "I thought you were younger." "I was younger but I'm younger no more. I'm sixteen going on seventeen." "When going on seventeen?" "Soon." "When soon?" "Three months. Three months and two weeks and a single day if you have to know. A Tuesday. June 15th." "I wasn't contradicting you." "They why you pumping me dry on it?" "No, you're sixteen, going on seventeen. Just small." "That's what I told you. I don't lie." "I wasn't accusing you of lying." "You were acting like it." "I wasn't even acting like it." "Then you were getting around to acting like it then." "I wasn't even doing that." "What's in the grass?" "Yes, you're old enough to see. But first I want to warn you about what it is so you won't get shocked." "I don't get shocked. Out of my way." He brushed me aside. Not hard, not light. And said "Good God, two heads. I think I know them too. No, I don't know them. They look like they're buried alive up to their heads." "That's the image I felt." "And kissing. Why would someone do that?" "Will you get the police for me now?" "You get them. I'll stand guard." "You won't touch them, move them an inch?" I said. "Who'd want to touch two dead heads?" "We can both get in big trouble if you do." "I said I won't. Just go." "And don't make it obvious to anyone else what we have hidden here. I don't think there should be a crowd." "I might look weird, but I'm not. I wouldn't want anyone else to see." "Then I'm going," I said. "Whatever you do, please don't stay on my account."

I'm looking out the window. It's the nice time of the day. The only time around now where the sun shines through into my apartment. So I like to be at the window if I can and take it in on my face. So I'm at the window. Taking in the sun. It seems very cold out. People in their heaviest coats. Cold breaths blowing before them when they walk and talk. Dripping mist on my glass. When I see an old man push a young man and the young man push the old man back. Right down at the corner of the park at Fourth and Bridge. Oh oh, fight. Now they're pushing one another back and forth and even harder the next time till the young man knocks the old man down with a two-hand shove. I go to the phone. I didn't see who first started it, but if it was the old man knocking the young one down I don't think I'd complain. But the young people. When they start knocking the old ones down for any reason, look out. So I'm at the phone. Receiver in my hand and dialing Operator, but the phone seems dead. "Operator, Operator," I say into it but get no response. I click the phone clicker several times, which almost never works to get them, and still no response. I go back to the window. Two squad cars are already there, four policemen and a lady stepping out. Mental telepathy, I think. Or whatever, but who's the lady? The young man's mother? The old man's sister or wife? The young man's mother and old man's sister or wife? A policeman picks the old man up. He'd fallen on his back. Lucky it wasn't his face he'd fallen on, or if on his side, his hip that was hurt. He has eyeglasses. He's rubbing them, so they weren't broke. Then he points the glasses at the young man. The young man points his finger back. They both point at one another, then rush one another with their hands out as if they're going to strangle each other's necks. They're broken up by the police. Both men point farther into the park. All of them, police, two men and lady walk a few steps farther into the park and seem to surround a patch of ground and look down. The lady sort of collapses slowly to her knees, as if she didn't want to get them hurt. The old man stops her from falling sideways on her back. While he's still holding her on her knees, the old and young man shake hands. So all's forgiven there, at least temporarily, for I'm sure the police had something to do with that. The lady's helped to a police car by the old man, so maybe she is his sister or wife. She isn't the young man's mother, as he just stays with the police in that circle they're around, smoking very calmly his cigarette. A crowd forms. Some people I know, some I don't. Mrs. Riner. A notorious busybody, so of course she was the first to come. I can think what she's saying. Lots of questions. And is told and sort of showed by that young man, it seems, and scoots away holding her mouth as if if she didn't she'd lose it. What's going on? Now they got me curious. More squad cars. A green police truck. An ambulance and intern or hospital worker from it hurrying over with a black box. The police roping off the corner of the park and pushing back the crowd now as big as one for a fire. I'd like to go downstairs. I could go downstairs. Why don't I go downstairs? All it takes is a couple of sweaters and my coat and furry boots and hat and it's not going to be over by the time I get there. I put on my outside clothes and boots. I'm leaving the apartment when the phone rings. The phone's working, I think. I pick it up. It's my son. "How are you, Mom?" "Fine as usual," I say. "Just called to say hello and see how you're doing." "Doing fine, thank you." "Everything all right?" "Everything's about as usual, thank you." "Turned kind of cold again all of a sudden, wouldn't you say?" "It's still winter." "But it was so pleasant for a couple of days, almost shirt-sleeve weather, and then cold as anything when I left for work. I hate it." "I haven't been out yet so I don't know." "You should get out. If just for a walk around the block for exercise, even if it's cold." "I was on my way out when you called." "Am I holding you up?" "It'll wait." "You know, I called before and got this strange humming sound from your phone and no ringing. The operator, who I later asked to reach you since I couldn't, said your phone was out of order." "It was." "That's what she said. It made me worry a little. I knew if your phone was out of order for a long time, you'd let me know because you'd know I'd be a little worried if I called you for a long time and found your phone didn't work." "I would." "That's what I thought. I just wanted to make sure. But it made me worry a little." "You know the phone services these days." "I'll say." "Okay I'll let you

go now, Dan. And thank you for calling." "Take care, Mom." I
go downstairs.

"Mrs. Nichols?" "I know what it's for, officer." "Are you Mrs.
Nichols?" "Of course, and I know why you're here. Let me see
to my stove and I'll be right along with you." "We don't want you
getting upset, but it's about two of your tenants." "Mr. and Mrs.
James. Or Mr. James and Miss Abbot or whatever she began
calling herself then. Ms. She favored Ms. she told me. I know all
about it. In the park at River and Fourth Streets." "Bridge and
Fourth. I want to ask you a few questions." "Of course you do.
Sticking out like cabbages on a platter, Mrs. Solis said—I didn't
see the heads myself. Or like she said she thinks cabbages must
look like that when they grow on the ground. They weren't nice
people." "I'm going to show you some photographs we made. We
thought the trip to the morgue would be too grim for a person
to take." "Oh, I can take it. Those two—I had no personal at-
tachments to them. They gave me the rent, each one every other,
and if I was lucky around Christmas they said 'Hello, how are
you?' but mostly slipped it under the door. I didn't hate them,
mind you. They weren't nice people and they made lots of noise
with their music and parties and trouble for me against the
tenants and eventually the landlord against me and the tenants
against the landlord and me and then this building against the
next building and the city if you can believe it, till I didn't know
where it would end. And at first I was on their side. I'm a poor
working person also—everyone knows a super doesn't make
much. I get my rent and some extra dollars a month for bringing
out the garbage cans and channeling the tenants' complaints for
repairs I can't do. My husband did, but he absconded with a
month of rents, the police said—it's in your records—and never
was found or came back. The whole building's. The landlord was
kind enough to keep me on." "Look at these photographs, please."
"You don't have to show them to me. I know it's them." "I want
you to look at these photographs." "But I heard. Two people
alone in this building were at the park and saw the heads before
they were taken away. Mrs. Solis I mentioned and the Ballards'
son Tom." "Is this Miss Abbot, or Mrs. James as she was also
known as?" "They weren't married." "I know it's hard, Mrs. Nichols, but please look at this." "It's not hard. That's her." "And

is this Mr. James?" "He was the worst of the pair. Neither was nice, though I think she could have been, without him, but he was a troublemaker born through. His clothes—his beard—everything: he was a mess." "Is this him?" "No, that's not him." "This isn't your 2A tenant, Timothy James?" "Well I never saw him with his eyes closed so or hair combed." "Take one more look." "I'm looking and still don't see." "Would you mind then coming with me for a closer observation?" "Not at all." "You're not required to, you know." "Don't be silly. I'll get my coat and turn off the stove."

Let me just read to you how their letter ends. "To sum up, your son, Timothy J. Burns, was found dead with a female friend, both their heads surgically removed by an unknown assailant. Every means within our power has been employed and will continue to be employed in finding the killer or killers involved in this brutal crime, but so far with little success. You have our deepest regrets. And it is also only with our deepest regrets that we were unable to ascertain till now where Mr. Burns' family lived, for, unfortunately, there were no records of any kind in the city under Mr. Burns' surname, as he was known almost exclusively as Timothy X. James." It's addressed to both of them—that's how much they know. But how can I show it to him? One after the other, bing-bang, though actually Timothy's first, though his might as well be postdating Mom's with Dad theoretically just getting the news. I'm going to shelve it for now and let him think Tim's taken an extended vacation to one of his distant lands as he was always planning to and will one day be popping in on him soon with all sorts of souvenirs. Dad's not going to last much longer. And later on, when it comes to divvying up whatever's left of the estate and if there is any insurance on Tim, I'll drag out this old letter and explain to the lawyer and insurance company alike why I couldn't for Dad's sake submit it in to them till then. But what do you think? I can't go ahead without also your say-so, for no matter what you maintain, you're as much a member of this family as me.

"Mr. Hirsch?" "Yes." "Fine. I'm calling about your wife, Tina Hirsch, also going by Tina Abbot, Bettina or Tina Abbotman, Bettina or Tina or T. J. James." "Never James. That she only used to get their apartment and for welfare." "I'm calling about her.

I'm afraid I've bad news." "If you tell me she croaked, that's not bad news. If you tell me she almost croaked or was shot, butchered and raped but somehow survived, now that's bad news. Anything else about her but her final departing I don't want to hear. I am not responsible. Get that? I in fact took out one of those no-longer-responsible ads in our newspaper to that effect, and can get the date and page for you if you'll hold on. She left me. The courts know that. We're still legally married but legally separated and in three weeks' time will be legally divorced, with her having no legal rights to ever again see our kids. So I don't want to hear of her. Anything there is, phone my attorney, 362-1466. For to me and to the children, whatever you have to say about her, she's dead."

"You think that's bad? Shit. Once upon a time back, but you probably read it in the papers. Big stuff. But you never read the papers you say." "Never. Always give me books." "Well this was in the papers. Big mystery of the month. Do you like mysteries?" "That's the type of books. Those first and then space. Love them." "This was called the Doubleheader Case. Something about baseball at least, happening around when spring training was ending up or the regular season just begun I think. But that was me." "You were the Doubleheader?" "You heard of it?" "Of what? To this riddle, tell me the answer." "There were two unidentified heads. Me. Shot them. Cut them up into nitty-bitty pieces except for the heads. The nitty parts went down the johnnies and out the car windows and over the bridge free and clear. Here a piece, there a piece, everywhere a piece-piece—just like our old Uncle Mac. The two heads I took out in a knapsack and put them where they could be found near a baseball diamond in the park." "No hidden meaning intended?" "Why? And it wasn't I didn't like these kids. They seemed all right and I appreciated what they were trying to do, even though I couldn't help them." "I'm not really interested. Can I get back to my reading?" "Let me tell you, though, repeat a word of it and I swear you won't be around to yap again." "But I said I'm not interested. I've heard it all. I'm busy. I want to read. Heard all there is for a lifetime. I don't want to know anyone's secret secrets anymore, so don't tell me a thing." "But it's all right for you to blab on about yourself though." "You thought that was myself before with that dumb

slut? Hell, that was what I read in this book." "Show me where."
"It's there. Inside. How can I find it again? One of the pages. But
I only read it." "I thought so. But this couple. They lived around
the block. I'd seen them before. Very political people. Not like
they held jobs in politics. Just interested in improving the city
and country and enrolling people up for their new party and
starting strikes and all those political goings-on. So I visited
them one day, or rather they visited me." "Which was it?" "Remember: don't repeat anything of it." "Forget I asked." "They
visited me. I was home and they knocked and said will I join
up? Sure, baby, I said, I'll join anything, come on in and have
a good time. They had a petition they wanted me to sign. I said
have a shot of whiskey with me first. They said they were in a
hurry, had a thousand more names to sign up. She was very
pretty, glasses and all." "What's wrong with glasses?" "For you,
yes, but for a woman—well she was all right, I didn't complain."
"All my sisters wear glasses and one once even modeled for television in them." "I wasn't insulting your sisters. I'm sure they look
great in them." "People have such prejudices about the most
stupid things." "Anyway, I was, I have to admit, a bit drunk at
the time, and when she sat down—" "I have a cousin, for instance. Can't stand women with long straight hair. It gets him
right here every time. Frizzy hair, kinky or curly hair, any kind
of hair but long and straight. He says all women ought to have
short, wavy hair—that would be ideal. Or at least not past their
shoulders, but certainly not longer than that, and absolutely not
longer than that and straight. I said to him that's ridiculous. He
said no, women were not born to have long, straight hair. I told
him I never heard anyplace about women or men or anyone
where it says that. He said no, long, straight hair is only meant
to get men attracted to them and that's not what hair on women
was meant for."

THE ONLOOKER

His daughter puts her arms out, waves her hands, shakes her feet, wants to get out, so he unbuckles the strap around her, takes the shopping bag off the back of the stroller so the whole thing won't tip over when he takes her out, takes her out, stands her up, puts the bag on the seat and follows her with the stroller down a corridor of the mall.

"Stella, let's go in here a second," he says when he sees there's a sale going on in the classical record store, but she continues walking, looks back, wants to be chased her expression says, so he follows her, saying "I'm going to get you, I'm going to get you," she stops in front of an ice-cream store and looks at him. She wants to go in her expression says. "I'm sorry, we can't," he says. "Stella, don't! Come here!" She goes in. He leaves the stroller outside the store, goes in, takes her hand, she already has several small peppermint canes in her other hand. He holds out his hand, she drops the canes into it, he puts them into their box near the floor. He walks her outside the store, points the stroller to the record store, sets her behind the stroller so she can push it, she pushes it a few feet and then turns around and starts walking. A short man around seventy is looking at her, smiling. "She wants to go her own way," he says to Will.

"Always her own way. I want to go this way, she wants to go that. You always know which way I want to go by the opposite way she's going."

"Goodbye, goodbye," she says to the man, stopping to wave to him.

"What a cute doll." He goes over to her, puts his hand in front of her waving hand and waves to her. "Bye-bye, honey. But where you going bye-bye to? Home? Your mommy?"

"Goodbye, goodbye," and she goes down the corridor, stops, does a few dancing-in-place steps while looking at her shoes, says "Ishi, ishi," which is her word for feet, socks, boots and shoes, goes on. The man walks with Will behind her.

"How anybody would want to hit those kids," the man says.

"You mean parents? I'm sorry. Child abusers?"

"I've seen it on TV. A whole article about it. Parents, relatives, friends of the mother even. You know, living with them. Why would they?"

"The children are vulnerable. You beat her—what does she know? Not 'know,' but what can she say? She can't talk back and she can't tell anybody she's being beaten. So no one knows she is unless he sees the marks, which can be explained away by the beater as 'She fell'—something. Really, maybe not as simple as that, but the beater, for his or her own reasons, has to beat someone smaller than himself."

"It's awful. I can't understand it and I never will."

"Oh, I can. Child abusers, wife abusers—beat your wife, beat your kid. The beater's frustrated, things aren't going well, someone beat him or her as a kid. He can't work it out any other way, so he beats up his child or wife or both. Old people too in wheelchairs get beaten up by their families."

"That the program didn't say. It did mention the wives. But a baby! An old person like me you might get disgusted at. We can be a pain like them sometimes, but we're also ugly. But look at her. She could never be disgusting-looking. How old is she?"

"Fourteen months."

"Fourteen months. Why in the world anyone—even if they did want to, as the impulse must be there with every parent sometimes—"

"That's true."

"But why would they carry it out? That's what I don't understand. How could they? It's more than crazy."

Stella's going down another corridor. "Excuse me—you're probably right. —Stella, come here! —It is probably more complicated than we could ever know, but I better go after her. Going this way?"

"No, my store I'm going to's over there."

"Nice talking to you then."

"Bye-bye, Stella," he says.

She's standing outside the optician's door, pointing inside. "He's busy," Will says, going after her and waving goodbye to the man. "Don't go inside, sweetheart." She goes inside.

"Goodbye, goodbye," she says, going up to the optician.

He's sitting facing a woman at a small table, spraying the lenses of a pair of glasses with glass cleaner. "Ah, my steadiest customer. Come in for trifocals this time, Sarah?"

The woman turns around in her seat, smiles at Stella. Stella reaches for the glasses in his hand, says "Yeyes, yeyes."

"Stella, sweetheart, come with daddy," Will says and takes her hand and says to the optician "Thank you, sorry for the bother."

"*Stella.* That's right." He puts the glasses on the woman. "Look straight into my eyes," he says as Will takes Stella into the corridor.

She uses her other hand to pull her hand from Will's and goes back the way they came. He follows her with the stroller. She goes up to the side window of the bookstore at the end of the corridor, puts her hands and forehead on the glass and looks inside. Will stands behind her, sees the elderly man from before at a paperback rack about twenty feet past the narrow window. He's reading a book. Stella looks at Will, points to the man or just to the store or something in the store. "Yes, the man," Will says. She puts her head up against the glass again. The man has two paperbacks in his hand now, puts one back in the rack, quickly looks behind and in front of him, puts the other book into his side coat pocket and without looking at it makes sure the flap is over the pocket. Then he walks down the paperback aisle, looking at books, and starts for the door.

Will doesn't want the man to see them there if after he leaves the store he walks this way. He grabs Stella's hand to steer her toward the optician's, she waves her other hand to the man as he passes. He didn't seem to see them. "Goodbye, goodbye," she says. He stops, looks back at her, Will, then at the window they're in front of, turns around as Will nods at him and continues walking.

"We have to go now," Will says to her, taking her coat and sweater out of the shopping bag. He looks at the man. The man keeps walking, doesn't turn around. Will's on his knees. People pass them. Stella's flapping her hands and saying goodbye to them as Will's trying to get her arm through the sweater sleeve.

At home he tells his wife about the man.

"I think he's a child abuser," she says. "To what extent I can't say, or even if he is still one—but that's why he brought it up."

"I don't buy that. He didn't have anything of the abuser of any sort in his mannerisms or on his face."

"No. Being so small, he was probably picked on as a boy and maybe as an adult and maybe even still. So he lets or at one time let very little people have it—maybe his own children—when he got the chance."

"I think he was just a shoplifter. But not because he wanted to save money. He was too nicely dressed. For the thrill of it I'll say, or because he's a little crazy that way. As for child abuse, he was just a sad lonely guy who wanted to talk to someone and child abuse was the first subject he could think to talk about with me. Maybe, as he said, because of some TV program he saw recently about it, and also because he knew it'd be something I'd be interested in because I have a small child."

"You didn't think of reporting him to the bookstore?"

"Of course not. Would you have?"

"If he was a child abuser, yes. But if he was only a sad shoplifter as you think that's all he was, then I guess they can take the loss better than he can."

"That's a good way of putting it."

TRY AGAIN

I look back at what I did to her today and I know what I did was awful, just couldn't be worse, and I slam my fist into the pillow and cry. "I can't go on today," I say to her and she isn't talking to me and leaves the room almost as soon as she got in it and I follow her down the hall and say "I can't go on today, I feel miserable, I hate myself today, hate all life, especially mine, I suppose I'll feel differently tomorrow or some day, but speak to me, say something," and she puts on her jacket and hat and leaves the apartment. I run after her, past the door that's still open and yell down the stairs "Don't go, talk to me first, I'm sorry, sorry, how many times must I say I'm sorry for all the lousy things I did to you today and all the other days but especially today before you'll come back if only even momentarily and say 'Okay, what is it, why'd you do those things—once and for all, what makes you?'"

I run to the window and open it and see her stepping outside and I yell her name and she doesn't turn around or answer and I grab a flowerpot off the ledge and throw it to the sidewalk so it'll land a few feet in front of her and she'll look up and know something's wrong and that I only threw the pot to get her attention, that that's how desperate I am, and that she has to speak to me before I get even worse, but the pot lands on her head. I know she's dead. She just collapsed to the ground, pot splattering all ways, a big smack, crack, her head, the pot, I can't believe it and want to throw myself out the window. Instead I yell "Nooo," and tear a lamp out of the wall and throw it at the door and throw over a table and all the chairs around it and pick up one of those chairs and smash it against the end table and pick up the end table and smash it against the wall and beat my fists against the wall and stomp and scream and yell "Oh no," and run down the three flights shouting "It isn't, I didn't, oh my God, how could I have?" and see her on the sidewalk not moving, people have gathered around her, I say "I did it, I'm sorry, I only meant to attract her attention, we got into an argument, usually my aim is good, I only meant to throw it in front of her, we got into many arguments, I said something she didn't like this time, I've been lousy to her all day, week, all month really, but I never hit her before, it was so stupid of me to do, throwing that pot, never hit her with anything or threw anything at her before, not even a pillow, I swear it, I loved her, oh my God, she's got to be alive, got to, is she dead?"

"Dead," a man says. "I'm a doctor, retired now, and she's dead. Someone should call the police," he says to the people around him.

I run down the block, someone chases me, "Get that man, trip him, hold him, he just killed someone," he says.

"I didn't do it on purpose, honest, it was an accident," I yell at people I pass who just stand there, none running after me. The man tackles me, climbs on top of me, I say "Let go, I'm going to kill myself, I was running to the subway, I was going to throw myself under the wheels or on the third rail, whichever came first," and he says "Not till you had a proper hearing before the courts of law for what you did."

I throw him down and grab him from behind by his neck and stick my knee into his back and say "Don't follow me, please, you have to let me handle it my own way," and he says "You bastard, you killed her, she was such a pretty girl, I've seen her around, and nice, you're going to get thrown away for life soon as I grab you and hold you down for the police."

I say "Don't," and he says "I will," and I say "Then I'll have to hurt you to stop you from trying to grab me," and he says "You better do something before I get up and clip you so hard you can't run off again," and he starts to push himself up and throw me over and I squeeze his neck till some people grab me from behind but they must have grabbed me too late for he suddenly slumps and I let go and they lift me up and someone who's kneeling over him says "Holy gee, his heart's stopped," and starts breathing into his mouth. I kick and shake off the two men still holding me from behind and run for the subway or anyplace where I can kill myself.

A few people chase me now, one throws something at my feet, I trip, get up, there are three of them, two women and a man and I see an empty wine bottle at the curb and grab it and say "First one to touch me or try to stop me from what I've got to do to myself is going to get hurt, I swear to you, very hurt."

"What are you going to do to yourself?" the man says and I say "Throw myself under some subway wheels or the third rail," and he says "Under the third rail?" and I say "On it, whichever comes first," and he says "Hell you are, you're only going to try to get away so you can kill a third person and then a fourth," and lunges at the bottle and I smash it over his head, he falls down, half the bottle is still in my hand, the two women grab me and I stick the bottle into the chest of one and slam the other woman with my other hand and kick her head and body when she's down till she doesn't move. I start to run, look back, the three people are still down, a crowd's chasing me now, about twenty of them. I hear sirens, run into an alley I know thinking I can climb the wall and get away through the backyards. They follow me in. Wall's too high. I jump and jump. "Make way," a policeman says. Crowd parts. Two policemen, both with drawn guns. One gets on his knee and the other stands crouched and both point their guns at me and one says "Stay put, don't turn or move," and I say "Good," and turn to them and say "I'm going to get you guys with the knife in my pocket," and reach for it as I run at them and they fire. Bullets chip off the wall and pavement around me before one goes through my throat though I feel no pain. I'm on the ground but I don't remember falling there. Someone's searching my pockets and says "No knife." "Let me at the bastard," a man says and there's a commotion to my right and my eyes open and I see some people trying to stop a man from getting at me. They can't hold him and he comes straight for me. He's a big guy and has a hammer in his hand and the policemen step out of his way.

I wake up and Susie's up and I say to her "You wouldn't believe the dream I just had," and she says "What time is it?" and I say "Let me tell you about my dream first," and she says "Hold it, look, what's the time, it's on your side," and I say "8:35," and she says "8:35, why didn't you tell me?" and I say "I was asleep," and she says "I mean just now," and I say "So you're late for a change," and she says "I punched in late twice last week and they want to dock the time from my paycheck from now on," and I say "Let them," and she says "You're paying me for the lost time?" and I say "If they're going to be so cheap, whatever it is, I'll pay you, for how much could it be?" and she says "I still don't want to be late so many times, you get a bad name, they won't promote me, I want to do good at a job once and not be a loser like you all the time sleeping your life away in bed," and I say "Bed, right, listen, my dream," and she says "Will you shut up already with your dreams, I've got to go," and I grab her wrist and say "Just let me tell you, I want someone to hear it before I forget it," and she says "Write it down," and I say "I can't write things like that, I just want to say it," and she says "Write it down like it's a letter or notes and show it or tell me when I get home from work," and I say "It won't be the same, it's fresh in my mind now," and she says "Please, will you let go of me?" and I say "It'll only take two minutes, at the most three," and she says "Will you please just let go?" and I say "I'll make it one minute," and she says "Please, I'm getting mad," and I say "Less than one, time me, I promise," and she says "For the last time now, please let me go?" and I say "No," and she says "Diego," and I say "No," and let her go and she gets out of bed and leaves the room and I yell "You, whatever you are, just go screw yourself," and she yells from the hallway "Why?" and I yell "For not listening," and she yells from the bathroom "Then if you're going to be so stupid, go screw yourself too," and I yell "And you can just stick it up," and she says "Same from me to you, stick it up, but I haven't time for any stupid arguing with you now," and I yell "You haven't had time for a minute of listening either, you never listen, you hardly even talk with me anymore, you never do anything with me anymore, you barely sleep with me, goddamnit, so leave, goddamnit, or I'll leave," and she yells "All right, I'll leave," and slams the bathroom door and I yell "I didn't mean for always, I meant just for today," but she doesn't say anything and I go to the door and knock and she says "What?" and I say "I want you to know I didn't mean for one of us to leave for always, just for today," and she says "I can't hear you when the shower's on," and I say "The shower's not on," and then I hear the shower go on and I try to open the door and it's locked when it's usually not and I say "Will you let me in?" and she doesn't answer and I yell "Just say then you know I didn't mean that I want one of us to leave here forever or anything like that, I got hotheaded before, I'm sorry, all right?" and she says "I wasn't, I'm going, soon as I finish my shower I'm going to pack my things and take them to work with me and sleep over at a friend's place tonight and look for another apartment and come back for the rest of my things when I get my new apartment, I'm glad this finally happened and you should be too," and I say "I'm not and none of this would have happened if you had listened to my dream," and she says "Phooey on your dream," and I say "But that dream scared the hell out of me, you can't imagine, it was horrible, I was killing innocent people in the most barbarous ways possible and one of them was you," but she's turned the shower on more and I suppose didn't hear what I just said and I'm sure couldn't hear me now because she's flushing the toilet one time after the other and it doesn't seem she'll stop and I go to the bedroom and get dressed and she comes out and gets her overnight bag and throws some things into it and starts getting dressed and I say "Susie, I'm sorry," and she says nothing, keeps packing and I say "I'm very sorry, honestly, listen to me now," and she says "You said yourself it isn't working and it isn't, we've seen that, so let's forget it," and she puts on her shoes and heads for the door and I say "Really, it was the dream that made me upset, I mean it," and she says "I meant it too, I'm tired of the way we don't get along together, for the first few months it was all right but there's nothing good about it now, there's no fun, no talk, no good times, no surprises, no just about anything and whatever sex we have you seem to have exclusively because I just lay there and let you take it and I couldn't care, I don't want to share anything with you from now on, I can't, I am completely turned off by you and today capped it, the camel's straw, the broken back, it would have happened anyway, maybe tomorrow, maybe tonight, maybe in a week or month but I'm sure sooner, so be glad it happened if it was going to happen and it was going to, definitely, now rather than when it might have been tougher to take later, so goodbye," and she grabs the doorknob and I say "I can't take you leaving like this now," and she says "You better start taking it because I am leaving like this and now," and I say "Okay, I can take it but I don't want you to go, let's try and work it out by talking some more," and she opens the door and goes and I slam the door and open it and run into the hallway and see her rounding the stairwell below ours and I yell down "Susie, be reasonable, it was only the dream I had because I'd killed you in it that made me so upset before," and she keeps going downstairs and I run to the window and throw it open and she's stepping outside and I yell "Susie, god-damn you, listen to me, I want us to talk," and she goes left and I grab a flowerpot off the sill and think I'll throw it to get her attention, throw it way in front of her so it doesn't hit her but where she'll look up at me and maybe start thinking some new thought and then I think no, better not and I wait till she's a good ten yards to the left before I look down and see that no one's below and just let it drop, it smashes on the ground, she turns to where the pot dropped and looks up at me and shakes her head as if she never saw anyone so stupid or pitiable and I raise my shoulders and make some motion with my hand that the pot fell accidentally and she waves that I'm lying or crazy and turns and goes and I slam the window down hard as I can and the bottom pane breaks.

Soon after that the buzzer rings and I say into the intercom "Susie?" and a voice says "It's Mrs. Wright from the first floor front. If you had to throw your flowerpot through the window, I'd think you'd at least have the decency to come down and sweep it up."

BO

One day I'm just not in my right mind. That's about the best way I can put it. I might have felt pretty bad other days but this day on the subway I'm really feeling things aren't right in my head and I'm definitely not in my right mind. That's closer. I'll begin when and where. I'm heading uptown. The express. IND. Months ago. Heading to my girlfriend's house. Not a girl, a woman. Her daughter's the girl. I got my valise for the weekend. My rough work clothes, my good clothes and the clothes I got on. Also some shorts and sneakers in the valise so I can run once a day the two days I'll be there. I'm going to help on her house. Fix up the basement with her. Plaster the floor, point up the brick walls as she says. What do I know from pointing? On the phone the night before she told me. Got a call from her. Big surprise: "Come up, all is forgiven, I love you very much. You must hate me by now the way I go back and forth in my emotions with you, but now I know how wrong I was and that you're the man for me. Leonore misses you too." Leonore's her daughter. I call her Lee. So does her dad. "All right," I said, "all is forgiven, and probably forgotten. I love you very much too, so when should I come up?"

"Right now if it was possible. But you won't take off unless you're really sick, so come up tomorrow after work."

"All right. I'll catch the 6:10 bus."

"Just take the subway to the bus station and I'll drive down and pick you up there."

"Why bother? I'll take the bus from the bus station and be in your cute little town by seven."

That's what it is. Cute. She too. Her daughter also. Their house, the town, the main street and surrounding countryside, all cute. "Till then, sweetheart," and I said "Same here," but felt a little as if I didn't know if I was doing the right thing going up there. I'd thought it was over between us. Glad it's not. All right, I'll go. I want to be with her. I love them both. So I go to sleep, to work the next day and half past five I'm on the A train that's to take me to the bus station at George Washington Bridge. But on the subway I suddenly feel peculiar. I don't know what it is or where from. People looking at me strangely, maybe me at them too. The newspapers. Talk of war, other countries' wars, sex, murder, scandals, gossip, all kinds of statistics and reports. People reading. Magazines too. The subway ads seem strange and horrible to me too. Everyone seems exhausted. Everything seems stupid and inhuman, like none of us should or don't belong. Like I especially don't belong. Subway rocking side to side. Screeching noises of passing trains and our train and whistles too. People pushing, some don't. Getting off, on. I'm standing. Need a seat. None. Crowded. I'm feeling crowded in by everyone and it seems everything and I almost want to scream. I hold one back. I'm feeling scared. The subway. Where's it going? Uptown the passing local stations say. Where am I going? Rochelle's, or I'm not so sure. I'm sweating: back, neck and face. I wish I was there already where I'm going. Rochelle's, but I don't know if I belong there now. With her. Here. Anywhere in the world in fact. I have to get off. Maybe it's some different kind of flu. I better wait till the train stops. It stops. I run upstairs. It's not the bus-station stop. That one I know where everyone from the front cars jam themselves in to get on the bus-station stairs. I have to call someone. I get the wrong number.

"No Rochelle here. What number you want?"

"I forget."

"Did you know what number when you dialed?"

"I'm not too sure."

"No wonder you got the wrong number. Please don't call again?"

"How can I if I don't know your number?"

"Right."

"I'm sorry. I'm not feeling too good right now, honestly. I was calling a friend for help." But he's hung up. I go through my wallet. I can't find her number. I always had it memorized. I know the area code is 914. Once I wrote her number down. When I first met her. On a library card. Now I remember. That I wrote it down. But that library card expired. I got a new one last year. Didn't put her number on the new one because I remembered it by then. Whose? Rochelle's? Rochelle Parker. 122 West Milner Street, Piermont, New York. I dial Information. I give Information Rochelle's name, address and town. She tells me to dial out-of-town Information and gives me the number. I do. I get her number. I get Rochelle. "Rochelle, something crazy has happened. I suddenly feel all mixed up and so out of it you wouldn't believe it and I don't know why. Please come and get me."

"What's wrong?"

"I just told you. My head. I feel crazy."

"You do sound a little crazy. You aren't joking? You're not calling from town?"

"I'm on 168th Street. Please come. I'm not kidding."

"I will."

I give her the address. I'm sitting on the cover of a garbage can when she comes. My valise I must have left on the train. I don't care. Work clothes, good clothes, as long as I got some clothes on. I get in the car and she drives. She says "What's wrong?" "Rochelle," I say, hugging her at a stoplight, wanting to be held. She takes me to her home, puts me to bed. I stay there for two days. Lee's away with her dad and his new wife. Rochelle feeds me broth, tea and toast, says it's probably only a very bad Asian-type flu I have which sometimes does weird things to the mind. "That's what I think too," but by Sunday she says "Maybe we're both wrong." She takes me to her G.P. He examines and talks to me and recommends a special public health hospital in the county. He calls and they say for me to come by later that afternoon. Just before we leave for the hospital, Lee and her dad drive up to the house.

"You going so soon?"

"Afraid I have to."

"But you never go till Monday morning. And Dad got me two new card decks so you and I can play Spit."

"I'll explain later," Rochelle says to them both.

The two admitting doctors ask me what I think is wrong. I tell them I don't know, it's tough to explain, I'm sure it started on the subway, but I don't feel as if I can go on with my life the way it is, at one point I thought it was just the world in general, the whole world, I don't know how other people are able to face it, but right now I can't. I feel terrible, not suicidal, just scared, confused, closed in, claustrophobic, strange feelings about everything in my head that make me sweat something awful and my body shake right down to my legs which I've never had anything quite like before. They say they understand. I say "You do?" Would I put myself in here for two to four weeks, maybe more, but a minimum of ten days? I look at Rochelle. She says "I think it's the best thing you can do." We kiss and she leaves. They give me drugs, a complete physical exam, a room to share with a very quiet man, want me to see a therapist twice a day just to speak. I tell her it suddenly came on me on the subway. She says it suddenly didn't and has probably been coming on for years, maybe since early childhood. "My childhood was great, so don't give me that." "You must have thought and still think your childhood was great and no doubt many parts of it were, but let's talk about it some more tomorrow, okay?"

We talk about my dead parents and older brother, who died in a bathtub. I say I loved all three very much. She says I may have loved them and very much but also could have feared them very much too. "Not true," I say, "as they never did anything like even raise a pinky finger to me to make me feel afraid." "Maybe you're right," she says, "or maybe you've forgotten or don't want to think about it and haven't wanted to for twenty or so years, but let's talk about it some more this evening, okay?"

About my ex-wife, child in Georgia, Rochelle, Lee, friends, schools, religion, work and sex habits. Past compulsions to get lots of attention, later desires for almost complete goody-good-iness and anonymity. "When did you change?" "When my brother passed out and drowned?" "That doesn't jell with what I've got down you already said and the chronology." "Then I don't know. Or I'm still not sure. But I don't care how much I'm not sweating anymore, I'm even more confused now than when I first came in here and don't see how all this talk's going to make me improve."

They put me on a special diet. Try another drug as the one

I've been taking turns out to be bad for my kidneys. Ask if I'll consent to staying a minimum of ten more days. I have to phone my boss and tell him I won't be coming in for two more weeks and he says then in that case he's going to have to let me go.

"All right then, you want to be unfair, be unfair. I'll be in this Monday nine on the nose."

"Tell you the truth, I got a new guy who does twice the job as you for a lot less starting money. And you took off too many sick days when I knew you didn't have to and weren't such a hot worker, so maybe you better not come back at all."

"Now you're making me mad. Everybody there knows I never took off when I wasn't absolutely dying, and for my extra over-time for the company I never once thought to be paid. Look, I've been told here to express my feelings more so I'm expressing them, for you know yourself you always said I was a hundred percent straight and honest and one of your hardest workers and for that praise I never had to ask. 'Damn good worker' were your damn words."

"You must've been hearing things then too. By the way, what's your room number so some of your former fellow employees can send you a bouquet?"

"What's that crack supposed to mean?"

"You don't like flowers? Then a joint card with all their signatures or maybe a basket of fruit. They told me to ask in case you had to stay."

"Nobody there wants to send me any card or fruit and you know it."

"They don't? I'll tell them that and you can be certain they won't. Take care of yourself, Bo."

"Sure, you give a damn. Just don't forget to put down that you fired me, you cheap bastard, for when I get out of here I want to walk into some unemployment checks."

"No skin off my pecker, tough guy, but for reasons of your kind of sickness or just any, I don't know if they give," and he hangs up.

Rochelle comes every other day around six. Sits with me. Says "You look better and seem to act better, you feel better too?" No. "Then you don't want to stay here longer?" Yes. I stay three more months. They give me plenty of pills, see that I swallow them and hope I'll continue to take my prescribed medicine once I leave here, "though remember, don't mix them with alcohol or you can die." After the three months I don't feel that much better but think it's time to go. My hospital coverage is up. My ex-wife writes she's ready to get the court to take away all fatherly rights from me for either unsoundness of mind or non-support. Rochelle has already told me she met another man and I shouldn't try and contact her anymore, and nobody I know takes her visitor place. Lee sends me a handmade get-well card once a week right up until the time I leave.

"You know, you really aren't sufficiently cured yet," the therapist says and I say "What can I tell you—I haven't the money to stay."

"You can be readmitted involuntarily and become a ward of the state, which in residency terms means you'd have to stay here until we say you can go."

"No, I think from now on, with a more responsible and positive attitude and meaningful job and more openness to people and no expectations about what I deserve out of life or preconceptions of what normalcy is . . ."

I'm given a month's supply of medicine and names of a few free group sessions in the city and return to my old neighborhood. My furnished room's been rented and what belongings I have are with the super downstairs. "Keep them," I say. "For I think if I'm really going to change my way of living and looking at things, I'm going to need a new apartment in another setting with better furnishings and wardrobe."

"If you change your mind by tomorrow morning, they'll be out front on the street."

I call up a friend. "Bobo, how are you, I heard what happened, tough luck, pal, as we always thought you were sitting on top of the world and had it made."

"Truth is, I'm still not sure how it happened, but I think I know how it won't again. I'm looking for a place to stay for a short while till I get back on my feet."

"You want me to put you up here?"

"I'll be direct; that's what I had in mind."

"Can't do. Booked solid with sweethearts all this week. Why don't you try Ken?"

Ken and Mary. Of course. Nice couple. Old friends. Ken says, "Fine with me, let me speak to Mary." Comes back on the phone: "She says no deal."

"Okay. No problem."

"It's nothing to do with where you been. She's still got this gripe against you for the way you treated Claire."

"What do you mean? Claire slept around and kicked me out of the house and wanted the divorce, not me."

"Listen, they speak on the phone. It's not only your missing kid payments for most of the year, but also the slow, subtle and maybe unintentional way Claire says you nearly drove her mad. She's got the shrink bills and mental bruises to prove it. Even your little girl had to go to one for a child."

"Could be true. Maybe I forgot how bad I was or like they say, repressed it so I'd forget. But I've already sent them most of my cash, just as I'm going to make good on all my old debts and not return to my mistakes and alibis of the past, so believe me everything's going to work out great for me and tell Mary I can understand how she feels."

"That's the spirit. Look, try Burleigh. His lodger left last week."

I phone Burleigh. Says "Sure, for one-fifty a month."

"I'm broke. Give me time to get a job and pay."

"Money on the line, Bo—I've got to live off what I get for rent. If it's not you then from a singles renting agency I can get a guy or girl for two and a half bills a month."

Several other people. Finally a friend of a friend who I heard might be renting says I can sleep on the floor for the night, but that's the best she can do.

Following day I'm out early looking for work. "In these times? Where you been? Factories are folding left and right or moving out of here, city's in hock up to its ears. Take a dishwasher job if you can find one, because with your skills, experience and education, that's about the best you'll get for the next two years." Unemployment says "If you are eligible for insurance, not for another three weeks." She wants me to fill out more forms. I say "Just a second, got to go to the men's room," stomachful of nerves from the lines and ugly walls and all her questions and suspicions and I leave the building through the rear. I'm in a spot.

Few dollars in my wallet. No likeable relatives with spare beds or money, friends with anything to lend. I get on the subway to try and convince that woman to let me stay two more nights on her floor. Suddenly I'm confused. Difficult to explain. Short of breath. I take two of my pills dry as I was told to do with outside emergencies when I'm feeling this distressed. For a few seconds I think they're stuck in my windpipe and try coughing them up. "Ach! Ach!" People looking at me with that look what's with him? Newspapers, magazines. Not so sure where I'm heading or presently am. Rush hour and with each door closing we're more crammed in. Horrible photos of victims, survivors, oppressors, refugees. Local passing stations going the opposite way I want telling me I'm traveling uptown. Next ride's a long one and when we stop I shove my way out to slap my face and blow my nose and breathe. Bags? Have any? On the platform I say "Say, buddy, not so fast, will you, for can you tell me—" but he runs upstairs. "Miss?" She too. Now nobody. I sit on a bench. Station attendant approaches same time as the next express. He says something but I don't hear him past the train's screeching wheels. Broom and dustpan with a long stick at the end of it, sweeping up wrappers and papers, dumping everything into the trash can by my bench. Doors open, close, people breeze by, platform empty again, then quickly filling up.

"Anything the matter?" he says.

"Ah, so you noticed."

"Too much to drink?"

"Too much of everything, but not drink. I can't."

"Bad news if that was to me happening," and he laughs and sweeps.

"I'm actually saying," but I'll be brief. He: "What's it then, drugs?" Me: "Drugs, yes, but hospital drugs for a manic depressed." Talk of drugs leads to thoughts of where I got them. After a long discussion about our mutual social and psychological problems and many of them similar, I ask him to call the hospital, give him the number from my head and change. He says on the phone "This the hospital? Not a hospital. Not a hospital," to me.

"Whose number I give?"

"What number is this? The man who told me to call wants

to know. Who's the man? Person wants to know who you are."
I give my name. He gives it and says to me "Says to put you on."

"Bo, this is Rochelle. What are you up to now?"

But I said I'd be brief. She eventually comes to get me. First
she says "Why'd you call?" I say "I was calling the hospital to
go back." Operator wants more change. Neither the attendant or
I have it so Rochelle takes the number and calls back. For a while
we can't speak because of the train noise. "I said would you
please come here to drive me to the hospital?" The attendant
tells her how to get to the station once she's on either deck of
the George Washington Bridge. In an hour she's come. Hugs me,
won't let me kiss her, says "Car's double-parked so let's make
it quick."

Takes my arm and we go. Her boyfriend's behind the wheel.
Once across the bridge and on the parkway I say "I'm really
feeling much better now and don't want to be any more of an
inconvenience, so why don't you let me off right here?" He says
"We phoned the hospital after Rochelle spoke to you before and
they said to bring you up there as soon as we can."

"Well that's what you're doing then."

"You don't think it's for the best?" she says.

"I'm sleepy, Rochelle."

Next thing I know she's tapping me on the shoulder as we
arrive.

JOE

Memory of it starts with them stepping off the train, then standing alongside it, conductor near them, same uniform it seems train conductors have always worn, gray cold day, cold gray day, but that's the way he always pictured it, contrast of the dark train and gray backdrop, his mother looking this way and that with an expression what's she supposed to do now? She told him to sit on the bench inside the station while she looked for a cab. Next thing he remembers they're sitting at a luncheonette counter in town, which they must have walked to for through the window he can see the train station across the street. While he ate she called a few taxi services in town but no cabs were available. It was wartime, gas shortage, gas rationed, scarcity of cars, cabs were considered a luxury out here, she was told, two of the three taxi services listed in the phonebook weren't even in business anymore. Most of that he got from talking about it with her years later though never telling her the main reason he was interested in the trip so much. There was about an hour, a half-hour, during it when he can't remember ever having felt so close to her. The counterman said the one operating taxi service would take her if she were a local or a regular customer off the train, but since she just spoke to them it was too late for that. Two men seated at the end of the counter near the wall phone asked if they could help her. She told them what she'd come out for. First a trip to a gas station several miles out of town to show the people there a photo of a dog and ask

if they've seen it around since he jumped out of a car there a
month ago. Then to the local dog pound to look for the dog. They
said they'd take her and the boy, no charge except for the cost
of the gas and maybe if they could bum a few cigarettes off her.
She said no really, that was too kind, but they could certainly
have the cigarettes. They said it's okay, they've nothing doing at
the moment, just so long as she doesn't spend all day at the
garage and knows they're going to leave her at the pound; it'll
only be a mile walk back along the boulevard to the train station
if she can't get a cab or another hitch. Next thing he knows he's
walking beside his mother, his hand in hers, across the street
to the corner where the car's parked. Next thing after that he's
in the back seat and the men in front. When the car was pulling
away from the curb the driver quickly rolled down his window
and spoke to a man running up to him, either a policeman or
someone in the army or marines. Their conversation was jovial,
seemed to go on for minutes, then the man outside waved goodbye to the men in the car and bent down to where his face almost
touched the back side window and smiled and waved to Howard,
who was right behind the driver. By this time there was lots of
cigarette smoke in the car, from his mother and the two men,
but it didn't seem to bother him. Maybe because of the fresh air
from the opened windows, maybe something else. He wondered
how the two men were able to fit in front. Only because his
mother and he were so crowded in back. Was the front wider
than the back? He didn't see how, still doesn't, but at least not
by that much, for the men were big and there seemed to be plenty
of space between them and between each man and his door.
When they started driving he thought the men might be bad men
who were going to do something awful to them. Kiss his mother,
steal her pocketbook, kill them both. She must have sensed what
he was feeling for soon after she patted his hand and said don't
worry, it's going to be a nice trip and I hope we find Joe. But
sitting in back with his mother. This part of the trip has come
back to him many times, maybe even a hundred, when no other
part of it has. In fact, to get to think of any other part of it,
it almost always comes after he thinks of this. Pressed close to
her, the scratchiness of her wool jacket or coat, her arm around
him, other hand stroking his hair, part of the way his head on

her lap, cool silk or rayon dress or skirt, her hard leg his head rested on, hand stroking his cheek and the back of his neck, he even thinks he remembers her leaning over and kissing the top of his head, but most of all his eyes closed and his head and torso squeezed against her side and her arm around his shoulder or back and other hand smoothing his forehead and running through and curlicuing his hair. They'd been alone outside lots of times in different places. She once took him to a movie at night. They sat in the mezzanine and he was allowed to find the men's room by himself and then to choose any one candy he liked from the two candy machines. All the times she took him to Indian Walk for shoes and after that to Schrafft's, where she'd let him pocket a few sugar packets and he'd have a vanilla ice cream soda and have to sit on a phone book to reach the straws. Cabs to several places, usually the doctor's. But they've never, he believes, been alone together in so enclosed and cramped a space. He's saying maybe that's the reason, helped it happen, or maybe it was also something else at the time that made her act to him the way she did. Maybe even the cigarette smoke had something to do with it, for them both; he just doesn't know. They must have gotten out of the car at the gas station, but he's never remembered it. When he's talked about it with her she's said she doesn't remember any gas station, just the train and dog pound and quite possibly the luncheonette, which does strike a bell, maybe from all the times he's mentioned it—"Though if that was the case," she's said, "I don't see why not the gas station too"— but she can't say they were there for sure. So maybe she changed her mind about going to the gas station or the men suddenly didn't have enough time for both the gas station and pound or else convinced her not to go: that it was silly, for example, to think the dog would go back there once it escaped. During the drive the men turned around every so often to ask her questions and she answered them gaily. He remembers smoke pouring out of her mouth and nose when she laughed and spoke. Actually, he doesn't know how accurate that memory is. It could have come from lots of other times, for she always smoked and spoke a lot and at the time laughed a lot too. She was having a good time though. That he definitely recalls. She smiled and laughed like the times when his father put his hand around her waist and planted a kiss on her cheek or grabbed her around the shoulder and with his eyes open kissed her lips hard or when he grabbed her waist and hand when there was some radio or Victrola music on and did a couple of dance steps or twirls with her or when he teased her in front of the children, all this was in front of the children, or said something about how beautiful their mother was or what a great figure she still had, though he usually jokingly called it "figer." He felt cold in the car—probably because of the opened windows for the smoke—and putting her arm around him and their bodies so close made him warm and probably made her warmer too. He doesn't know why they waited a month before going out there to look for Joe. Phone calls to the gas station and pound and man who lost Joe were made but that was all. His guess is that he badgered her till she gave in or she thought that after a month of him being depressed about it, only going out there to look for Joe would make him feel better. She's said "I suppose we went out there when we did because it was the earliest I could find time for it." "I know we got a cab to the pound," she's said, "and I'm almost positive it was from the train station. Though I might have gone to the luncheonette to call for it, but there were certainly no men." "Well I definitely remember them," he's said. "Two of them in the car, that they were young, the car old and leather-smelling till you all started smoking. Big bushy hair on one of the men. I forget the other's hair and I can't say whether the driver or guy beside him had the bushy hair—I think the driver. Maybe the car was actually a cab and the driver was a cabby and the guy beside him a friend going along for the ride or a passenger going in the same direction as us but getting off last. And this passenger or friend was the one with the bushy hair and the driver's I never remembered because I couldn't see it under the cabby's cap. And the uniformed man hurrying over could have been a fellow cabby and the uniform I saw might have only been his cabby's cap. Or else he wore it to complete what I think was sort of the standard cabby's uniform then and that was with a waist-length yellow jacket, leather or cloth, though maybe I got the color wrong and even the material and design. But what's it matter really? And it also wouldn't account for the luncheonette I swear we met those two men in. Maybe the driver and his friend were having lunch at the time and one of the cab companies you called from the train station, you say—the only one you said was still in business because of gas rationing and no new cars being made— or even from the luncheonette, if let's say the phones at the station were tied up and we crossed the street to call from there— said if you want a cab you'll find their one available driver having lunch this very moment at the luncheonette across from the train station, or the same one you're in. Or maybe we went in there to call for a cab or have a bite before we did and met the cabby by accident. But all of us sitting at the counter for at least a few minutes—so maybe you and I didn't have lunch there or even a snack, though I could almost swear the men had plates and coffee cups in saucers in front of them. Then walking to the corner where the cab or private car was parked. And the pudgy uniformed cabby or policeman or soldier hurrying over to the driver's window right after the car pulled out, and the man waving goodbye to me good-naturedly though that might be an embellishment, his smile and bending down to me to wave; still, it stays. But without question the cab or car ride, long or short, to the dog pound, which I might have slept part of the way through, so comfortable and close was I in the back with you, even if my head was lying on or up against what I remember as your itchy jacket or coat, which normally would have kept me awake." They went to the pound. Neither recalls how they got back to the train station, though she thinks she told the cabby that took them there to wait. "That's what I'd usually do in a situation like that and in an area I wasn't familiar with. And cabs were cheap then and the waiting period particularly, or else I called for another cab from the pound. For sure we didn't walk." The man at the pound said it was unlikely their dog was there, she said, after so long and especially since the last time she called him about it, but he'd show them around. They went into a large airy room with about forty cages with dogs in them and a few cats. They walked down one aisle and back along the other. None of the dogs looked at all like Joe. Then he heard a dog barking from behind a wall. "Listen," he said, and listened. "That's Joe." "Don't be silly," his mother said. "This gentleman will tell you: if he's not in this room, he's not here." "That's Joe, I'm saying— coming from through there. I know how he barks. He knows I'm here—must have smelled and heard me—and wants me to come get him." The man said the next room was where they kept animals that had recently been brought in. "If they don't show any signs of illness or anything, we let them in here. I know not one of them even remotely resembles an Airedale." "It's him, don't tell me," Howard yelled and started for the door to the room. "Just to amuse him could you let him in there?" she must have said something like. She doesn't remember saying it, neither does he, but it's what he thinks she would have said from the picture in his head of her at that moment. They went in. It was a small room with no windows and only a little artificial light. Four or five dogs in cages on tables and they all started barking when they came in. "At least we looked," she said outside the pound. He wanted to go to another. Said something like "Joe was a great runner and could have run twenty, even fifty miles in one day from where he jumped out of the car." She said they've done enough to find Joe today, that she's already called every pound on Long Island twice but would call each of them a last time this week, but that they now have to catch a train so she can get home in time to do some other important things, and so as far as she's concerned the matter's closed for the day. If she said that in those words he probably said what does she mean when she says a matter's closed? He probably also cried but stopped in a minute or two or just quietly sobbed but went along with whatever she said. He doesn't remember any part of the trip back or anything more about that day or ever thinking of doing anything to find Joe again. Memory of it ends with them in front of the pound, wide gray sky behind her. He assumes the whole trip took about six hours and that it was dark when they got home.

NEXT

They speak about me.

"Leg's a mess," crouched one says.

"You see his other shoe?" standing one says.

Or the same one says. No, they're speaking about me. Looking at me. Two figures. Two people. Men, I assume. Not two ladies yet. Ladies don't work so much in the subway system yet. As cashiers perhaps. Coin tellers? Not cashiers. Not coin tellers. What are they called, those ladies and gentlemen who take my money and give tokens and change in exchange? Or just give tokens or a token if I've given them the exact change?

But I'm not there. Getting tokens, giving change. Saying Good morning or Have a nice day, which used to puzzle or please them most times. Ten-dollar bill's the limit, their sign said. Mostly transistor radio music or news from inside their booth or cage. In the summer, baseball. Fall weekends, football. Nights, I don't know. And once one with a beard with classical music tuned in. But I'm not there again.

I'm between the tracks. Being picked up. On something.

"Jumped."

"Pushed," the other carrier says. "I'm not accusing anybody. Just that people do get pushed."

"Accidentally also."

"It isn't a rush hour."

"Doesn't have to be a rush hour for someone to get pushed on the tracks. People down here are always running."

"Oh, all people?"

"Some. Half. A few then. Running to catch a train that hasn't come yet. That's maybe three stations away and for all they know broken down. And this passenger probably near the platform edge like they're all warned not to and got bumped off by mistake."

"Will you two move him along?" a third voice says. "We got to get this line operating again."

I'm being carried. Lifted to the platform on that something I'm on. A litter. Two men lifting me to two men. I can see them now. Policemen are here. A woman in white. Probably a hospital doctor. Emergency. The young ones. Not practicing in a private office yet. What are they called? Coin tellers? Cashiers? Was my mind run over?

"Leg looks very bad," she says. The intern. That's it.

"We couldn't find his other shoe."

"Forget the other shoe. Gently. Easier. His internals. He hasn't been thoroughly examined yet."

"But the way he's dressed, those could be his only pair," the policeman says. No, one of the men who carried me from the tracks. Where a train hit me. I was hit. Pushed. Bumped? Did I jump? I forget. I was standing on the platform. Reading a newspaper. Heard the train's whistle. Looked. No, extended my head. Leaned it forward. My head. And looked in the tunnel at the train coming to the station I was at. It wasn't three stations away, broken down. And it wasn't the tunnel coming to the station I was at. I was looking, extending, leaning forward. My head. My whole body. Half. Waist upward. Sideward. Trackward. Newspaper in hand. Folded. To what story? Crisis declared? President said this, did that. The train. Train story. Two headlights like headlights from a car. Automobile car. Whistling. Unlike a car. Coming. I even saw two children in the front window of that first car looking at the station the train they were on was approaching. But where was I? Still on the platform. Head and half a whole body extended trackward. Seeing the train approaching the platform of the station I was at. When what? Something happened.

"Here we go, mister. You'll be in emergency in a jiff."

I'm being carried upstairs to the upper platform. Upper platform's for uptown locals. Lower's for locals going downtown. So

I was going downtown or on the downtown platform for what? Extending my head to the left. Downtown trains come from uptown to the left. Though it hadn't reached the platform yet. Still in the tunnel. Headlights. Long whistle. So I was there at the edge of the extreme left of the station where the platform and tunnel meet. Two boys' faces. Children. Could have been girls. Pointing. A girl and a boy. Dark hair, light faces. Suddenly the conductor in his front-car compartment looking alarmed and shouting Stop.

"Light as a feather," the front carrier says.

"To me he weighs a ton."

"You ought to take your vitamins then."

"Say, did you see that vitamin article in the newspaper yesterday?"

"Two days ago. I've been taking them for years. Megadoses of vitamin C. That's why my hair's so thick."

"It didn't say anything about hair that I read."

"Hair loss. I also don't get colds. But I was losing mine in patches. My pillow. Every morning. Then my brother said his brother-in-law had the same problem and someone told him of an article they read where vitamin C stops hair loss and restores a lot of what you lost. Look at my hair now."

"I know what it looks like."

"But it's the hair's body. I'd let you feel it if we weren't carrying this man."

"Later."

"Easy, you guys," the intern says. We pass a change booth. Whatever they're called they're in. Those token people. A token person sets down his bucket beneath a turnstile.

"Good luck, brother," he says, leaning over me.

Must be collecting. But that was nice. And how come I didn't hear the chang of tokens against metal? Before that, metal against the floor. How come I hear nothing but voices, no other sounds? No footprints. Shoe sounds. My sounds. No pain. She gave me a shot. I'm heading for the stairs to the outside. We are. Outside is light. It isn't night. I didn't know. I'm not on my own two feet. In my own two shoes. Stand up and be counted, brother. Who used to say that? Put your shoes on, Lucy, you're a big girl now. Who sang that? When I used to listen to such songs. But my shoe. What they say happened to it? Did they ever find it? Will I now only need one? That's no joke. Let me see. What exactly happened to me before? Put yourself in the other person's shoes. My father, my mother. I'm looking left. Was. Then. What? Jostled? Pushed? Bumped? Did I jump again? Did I ever jump? Years ago. So what. When I was a teen. Melancholic kid then. In college but mostly out. Jumped. Fell right between the well. Train went over me. Never touched. I got up. When I was this teen. Up, and I said, after the train passed over me. Stopped to exchange with passengers above me. The conductor mustn't have seen me and if he did, kept his mouth shut. But I got up and looked at the train leaving the station and said from the well Never again. Hallelujah and Handel's chorus and never again. A man washing down the tiles of the platform said Hey, you nuts? What are you doing on the tracks? I said then I was lucky. To the man. And that something's got to be going good for me all right. Because I didn't want to die. I said all that. Why'd I do it then? Love? Depressed and no foreseeable prospects that I could foreseeably see and in love with a loveless love? That was then. What about today? Did I? Jump? Same reasons? Similar? Did I plan it? Was that what was in my mind? No, my shoe.

Sidewalk, sunshine and street. A pedestrian audience.

"What happened?"

"Jumped in front of a train."

"She says he was pushed."

"She was there?"

"He looks bad."

"You wouldn't look good."

"But do you see his face?"

"Don't look."

"I can't help but look."

"You can turn around."

"Turn me around."

"Bastards."

"Who?"

"Whoever pushed him."

"You don't want to say things without proof."

"All I'm saying's what he said."

"I didn't say it. She did."

"Make way," my policeman says.

I'm slid into an ambulance. Doors locked. Suddenly sound-less, like a museum tomb. Blanket covering me. Correction. Egyptian. Addition. Can't tell from hot or cold, so what's the difference?

"How you doing, sir?" the doctor says. "You okay?"

What do you want me to say?

Driven off. Though red lights. Truckmen. Busmen. Whole world round pausing in mourning for me. A king out there would have to stop. If I were a boy or that melancholic kid again I'd be enjoying the trip. But I'm hopelessly optimistic. Hoggishly opportunistic. They'll never take my leg. I could never take my life. So what's up, Doc? That's what I want to say to your okay. Leg going to go? Will it be a good hospital my leg goes in? Clean? Maybe this is a dream? Wake me. Wake up. Time to get ready for school. Can Johnny come out and play? He'll need all two legs. Johnny's actually my name. But did I only leave my shoe behind? Somebody laugh. No, they would have mentioned that. But leg looks bad. Heard people say. And leg means foot. Foot touches floor. I want to get to the very bottom of this, Doc. Isn't that a line from some movie or play? Radio show? All of those. Mysteries. Adventure yarns. Well I never liked mysteries or yarns of any kind. Whirrr, not that I can hear the siren and sudden stops.

"You'll be all right," person in white says. "What you do, jump?"

Me? You see it in my eyes? Let me reconstruct for you, lady doctor. Male nurse. Person who rides with people to hospitals holding their hands. Not that I've been to one as a patient myself. Never. Once. Glass in hand. Hand you're holding, same hand. Different finger. Big one. Bad cut. Big deal. Right to the bone, the doctor said. Right to the bone, I later liked to say. And said not a while back. To whom? A woman? Woman I see or saw. Name begins with a D. De, Da. Da, De. Held my hand too. Was examining the palm. Telling me my life present, future and all my civil wars. Till she came to the ringer fing. Who? Not you. That woman. De, Da; Di, Do. Black hair, short body. Saying Short life, big finger. Long scar, what happened? Accident when I was twelve, I said. Glass cut right to the bone.

"Beep your horn if the siren doesn't work."

"That creep still won't get out of the way."

"Bump him."

"Our fenders can get locked."

"All the drivers do it for me."

"They want to lose their jobs."

"Not if you do it lightly."

Black hair, lean body. Short break for fainting.

"Move it, goddamn you, you stupid driver. Can't you see we've an emergency in here?"

In a room. People in white working on me. Scratching. Tickling. Cut it out. Can't feel a thing. Other people working on other people on other tables in the room. Curtains. Some not. Some smells. Pillorying light. "Now, if you don't mind?"

"Brief," a doctor working over me says.

"Can you tell me what happened, John?" a policeman says.

I open my mouth. Do I speak? He looks at me. Is very close. Now they're scissoring. Injecting. His lips are implanted in my ear.

"I know this is a bad time, John. But no time like the present. It's only we got to know. Records. This report here. Sooner the better. For you. Maybe for everyone. We have to know if we should pursue. Investigate. Did you jump? Were you pushed? And if so, by who?"

I open my mouth.

"What? Once more, John. Give it a try."

I tell him. In my head, I tell him, I try. You see. I was standing on the platform. Newspaper in hand. Two in the bush. World's crush. Plane crash. Those were the three stories I was between reading before. When the plane came. The rains came. That was from a song. I saw the movie. First the show. Saw the lights. First the whistle. Train coming from uptown to down. That's when I jumped. No, I was pushed. Officer, I fell. Stumbled. Wain wumbled. Wind blew me onto the tracks. William Wind. Ye old bloke. I'm very light. Johnny Light Light Light. As a feather my father useta say.

"No sense out of him. His vocal cords touched too?"

"In shock."

"Of course."

All my clothes snibbled off.

I'm naked. I'm cold. Shock, who?

So there I was. Fifty Arabs on one side of me. Hundred cannibals on the other. Cliff with five-thousand-foot ravine in front. Pit of cannibal-eating alligators in my back. No place to go. No direction. Light as a feather my mother also used to say. If you were thrown off a building you'd float down instead of drop, my father would say. Way back. Don't say things like that, my mother said. To me? You're so skinny, my brother used to say, that when you stand sideways you can't be seen. No, my sister used to say. Sister and brother in hospitals too. Mother and father eaten by cannibals there too. I stayed by their beds. Hands on my heads. Watered their brows. Cheeks all of bone. That when you drink tomato juice, my sister said, you look like a thermometer. Sister laughed. That when you wear a red tie, she said. Brother laughed at what sister had said. Mother laughed at what sister had said and brother and sister were laughing at. And father because they all laughed. Now I'm last. In a hospital too.

"Got to clean the lesions first."

Sutures does someone say? Scalpel? I see the scalpel. I saw the movie. See how they run.

Thermometer, and they all laughed. Their heads off.

"That's no rattle. Let's get the machines on him."

"Wheel them in?"

"Wheel him too."

"Double e-ing. Calling a clear."

Bells. Bings. Blood transfusion. That's the sting going into my arm.

I jumped. Hey, copper, still around to hear?

Nah, I fell. Gad's honest treut.

I was pushed, the dirty rat. There's your plate of beans. And when I get out of this joint. For I'm going to beat this rap. As you see, I'm hopelessly attitudinistic. Hopelostly antivivisectionistic.

No, I was so thin. So light. Johnny L. L. Light. That's what I was thinking of before. That when I got on the scale the needle didn't move. My father. That's how you can get a weigh. My brother. My sister saying Wag drags with your raggity gags and my mother a bony-beaked comedian of ninety, brown bear burned

to white. I don't want to go and so I'm not going, she said, no
matter what my age. Here the shiny sonshine her only survivor.
Vitamin E. Dose of those once a day what'll save me, she said.
Vitamin C. There's what I should do about my falling hair other
than stepping out of the way. Vitamin D. Holding my short-lived
hand. I was fibbing before, she said. Trying to catch how you
react. You don't. Or I didn't. But I know nothing about palmistry
except this line and it means long life. And here's where your
lines of affection would be and your wrist as asthenic rascettes.

Actually, I was blown on the tracks. Like that newspaper.
Single sheet. Carving our way through corridors now, blood
stringing along. Yesterday's headlines making waves. Wind wound
down the subway entrance from two flights above. Same steps
I was later carried up on one of those rolling ambulance carts.
Steered along sidewalk and street. Doors slammed. Siren turned
on. Ambulance driven away. Hey, wait for me, I screamed. There's
something you forgot. Pigeons settled on my chest. Invalid-eating
dogs licked my paws. What are you doing lying on a stretcher
in the street? a woman said. Ambulance rode off without me,
I said. Oh, I saw that funny movie too. Harry? Cary? Darnit, sir,
who were those two stars again?

Another pillorying room. Semiprivate. Patient beside me
with a football helmet clamped to his head. Dots and dashes.
Blots of flashes. Lights, camera, action. I'm strapped on my back
to an analyzer. Scanner. Transponder. Spectrometer. Tape re-
corders. Television sets. Doctor, Doctor, I want to confess. I
jumped. Lost the faith. Depression. Born out of rejection. Objection. Sustained. Next witness. Take the stand. No thanks, I'll take
it when I leave. Order in the court. My dentist. Dentist will be
identified. There's the chiseler. Took me to the cleaners. So I took
him to small claims. Said Malfeasance and practice. That when
I walked downstairs from his office my new fillings popped out.
That's what the dentist my poppa said his patients never said.
Later my mother said they did. Pass me the V.E. Good prostho-
dontics your dentist but couldn't diagnose or heal. So it was my
father who uprooted me from the plat. Said Join us, you ole
rumbum. Order in the snort. No. My sis said Join me, come, come.
That was my lover. Sunday palmist. Once a week divining my
hand. No life, short feeling, she found. No, it was I. Wild pram

on the loose. Baby cawing and kicking inside when it was saved. Crowd gathered. Camera men came. They're shooting pictures of me below. First thing out of my groin's my foot. A transsexual breakthrough. Balls, the king said, if I had them I'd be queen. No. She said. We did. As kids. You're still a kid. That's what Vitamin D said. Had a bellyful of my changes. But this isn't her flat. No sunlight. No yellowing fern or smell of mint tea. I'm where? They're scissoring. Shearing. Shaving. Sweating. Swearing. Hemming. Mending. Hacking. Yakking. Everything. All the ings. The bings. The dings. The drops. I was dropped to the tracks. Train coming. Conductor screaming. His first fall? I was called to the tracks, I said to him as I fell. He said No or Oh but Stop. Boy and girl at front-car window standing watch. No, I flew onto the tracks. My fly flew. That was it. I had a strange calling. I wanted to unzip. Your fly can be better zippered when you stand than sit, my father used to say. When you sit and try and zip you are just about sitting on your zipper, he said. Yes, Dad, I said, when the zipper tag flew off and I lost my footing and fell on the tracks.

Ether, ether, I yell from the hospital bed. This table. Wherever I'm being worked over on. The pain.

"He spoke," the doctor, doctoress, sorceress says.

"More anesthetic," someone says. Milligrams. Microgams. Look at those gams. Some pair. "Mm's," the anesthesiologist says.

"More ether," I say. "The pain."

But I've seen the movie too.

In the end the patient dies.

We couldn't save him, the doctor says.

His heart, someone else says.

A sheet is thrown over my face.

Not thrown. Laid.

Not laid. Lain on my face.

Not lain. Placed. A sheet is placed on my face. I'm covered. A sheet was placed on my face and now covers my face.

Though I've never seen the movie from here.

Next.

Stories in this collection appeared in slightly different form in the following periodicals, to which the author and the publisher extend their thanks: "The Student" in *Mundus Artium;* "All Gone" in *Kansas Quarterly;* "On the Beach" in *Threepenny Review;* "The True Story" in *Confrontation;* "Capital Labor" in *Pendragon;* "Jackie" in *Periodical Lunch;* "The Batterer" in *Cream City Review* and *Ohio Journal;* "A Lack of Space" in *Ohio Journal;* "The Former World's Greatest Raw Green Pea Eater" in *Cake;* "Wrong Words" in *Appearances* and *Asylum;* "The Doctor" in *Confrontation;* "Heads" in *Florida Review;* "The Onlooker" in *City Paper* and *South Carolina Review;* "Try Again" in *Ambit* and *Chouteau Review;* "Bo" in *Asylum;* "Joe" in *Denver Quarterly;* and "Next" in *Remington Review.*